Cactus View Book Club

Murder in Surprise

Cactus View Book Club

Murder in Surprise

Crime Thriller

By

Mark R Beckner

Becknerbooks Publishing

First Edition: June 2025

ISBN: 978-1-7369607-8-3 (paperback)

Credits

Sally Beckner – Copy review and editing

Front Cover – Sally Beckner

Writing companion – Roxy

Preface

After retiring from the Boulder Police Department following 36 years in law enforcement, I began my new career as a writer of fictional crime dramas. My stories evolve from my imagination, as well as from my time as an investigator. While each story is fictional, the police and forensic work are based on reality. I rely on the knowledge and experiences gained over my long tenure and from continued interest in actual cases to add realism to my stories.

This book is my fifth crime thriller. The setting takes place in Surprise, Arizona, our winter home for five months of the year. My wife and I live in an active adult community, much like the one described in this fictional story.

The inspiration for this story came to me after attending a book club meeting to talk about my fourth book, Silent Waters, a murder mystery that takes place in Boulder, Colorado. The engaging interaction and interest shown by the women in the club inspired me to write a crime thriller centered around a book club in an adult community.

Follow along as Cactus View Book Club members become embroiled in the investigation of multiple homicides. Four murders, various suspects, and a book club in turmoil. Detectives Dan Baxter and Lou Begay must unravel the secrets hidden in the adult community of Cactus View.

Thank you so much for your support. Independent authors rely on readers who are willing to take a chance on our work. Finally, please leave me a review, as it would be much appreciated. It really helps. I hope you enjoy the story.

Please visit my website for additional information.

Becknerbooks.com

Email: becknerbooks@gmail.com

Other books by Mark R. Beckner: **Behind The Lies**;
Death From Desire; Naked Evidence; and Silent Waters

Chapter 1

It was mid-January in Arizona, and Sixty-eight-year-old Linda Riggs had spent the afternoon cleaning and preparing her home for that evening's book club meeting. Twice a month, the ladies of the Cactus View Book Club meet at 6:00 p.m. on a Wednesday to discuss their latest book reading. It was Linda's night to host the meeting, although, as the group leader, she hosted most of the meetings. She arranged chairs in her living room in a semi-circle to accommodate seven women. Linda had set the wine and glasses on the granite countertop, dividing the kitchen from the living room. Light snacks and freshly baked oatmeal cookies waited on the dining room table. Linda's husband, Ray, had left for the evening to play poker with some of his softball friends.

Cactus View is a picturesque fifty-five and older active adult residential community of about 18,000 residents in Surprise, Arizona, a northwestern suburb of the Phoenix metropolitan area. Cactus View sits on the west side of Surprise, nestled against the Sonoran Desert and close to the White Tank Mountain Regional Park of Maricopa County. The community caters to the needs and desires of older adults and retirees. Cactus View offers many activities, including three golf courses, tennis, softball, pickleball, three athletic clubs with swimming pools, and many special interest groups. A community hub serves as a place for eating, socializing, events, and other activities. Cactus and palm trees are plentiful throughout the community. Residents enjoy breathtaking views and glorious sunsets over the mountains to the west.

At 5:50 p.m., the first club member to arrive was Maritza Perez.

"Come on in, Maritza," said Linda. "You are the first to arrive. Would you like a glass of wine?"

"Yes, the red for me, please," replied Maritza.

As Linda was pouring the wine, several more ladies arrived. "Hi Mary, Sharon, Judy. Come on in. Let me know what you'd like to drink."

"White wine for me," answered Mary.

"Me too," said Sharon.

"Red for me," shouted Judy.

Soon, Katy Cullen and Emily Settlemire arrived.

"Listen up, everyone," announced Linda. "This is Emily Settlemire. She is relatively new to our retirement oasis. She likes to read books, and Judy recently invited her to join our group."

"Welcome to the group," said Sharon.

Katy leaned over and whispered in Sharon's ear, "Look at that fancy black dress Emily is wearing."

"Once everyone has a drink, please find a seat, and we will go through introductions for Emily," announced Linda. "And please grab a cookie or snack."

After everyone had settled into a chair, Linda started the meeting.

"Thank you all for coming tonight. As you know, we have a new member joining our group. You've briefly met Emily Settlemire. Thank you for joining us, Emily."

"It's my pleasure," replied Emily.

"I think it would be a good idea to go around the room and introduce ourselves and provide some background information for Emily," said Linda. "I will start. I'm Linda Riggs, and I've been part of this club for five years. We are primarily a book club, but as you will find out, we also get involved in other activities. Sometimes, we just have a ladies' night out. I'm sixty-eight years old and married to my husband, Ray. He's a retired electrician. Myself, I was an actress until about five years ago. I had some minor roles in several movies but mostly did character acting in plays and musicals. Now, I'm a member of our drama club, and I perform here in Cactus View. When Ray retired five years ago, we moved here from Oregon. We love all the activities this place offers."

"You are still an actress, Linda," said Maritza. "But now you are doing it for fun."

"I suppose," replied Linda. "Why don't you go next," suggested Linda as she motioned toward Maritza.

Maritza brushed back her dark hair. "I'm Maritza Perez, and I'm fifty-seven years old. I've only been living in Cactus View for three years. My husband, Ricardo, and I moved here from Michigan three years ago. I was a corporate secretary, and my husband was an attorney. Well, my husband is still a part-time attorney here in Surprise. We have three children and five grandchildren. We came here to escape the cold

Michigan winters. I joined this group because I love to read, especially crime mysteries. I also enjoy pickleball, bocce ball, and the photo club."

"Thank you, Maritza," said Linda. "Who's next?"

"I'll go," said Katy. "Welcome to the club, Emily."

Emily nodded, "Thank you."

Katy continued. "I'm Katy Cullen, and I'm sixty-seven now. I retired at sixty-five as a lab technician at a pharmaceutical company in Colorado two years ago. My husband is Jerry, a retired financial manager. We moved here after I left my job, and we both love this community. I'm also a member of the Art Club. My specialty is painting landscapes. I joined this book club to make new friends and because I like to read and share my thoughts with others."

"Who's next?" asked Linda.

"My name is Mary Hipple," said Mary. "I'm sixty-two and spent most of my time raising our four children. I now have three grandchildren. My home is in Minnesota, but after my husband sold his construction business, he moved us down here. It's been a struggle, but I like this group because you are all so supportive."

"You don't sound too happy to be here," replied Emily.

"Well, my husband forced me to move here," Mary said quietly. "I have an elderly mother who could use my help, and I miss my kids."

"I'm sorry to hear that," said Emily.

"Your turn, Sharon," said Linda.

"Welcome to the club, Emily. I'm Sharon Jansen, the youngster of the group at seventy-seven."

Several members chuckled. Sharon continued. "You can probably tell from my white hair. Anyway, I've been in Cactus View for twelve years now. My husband, Charles, and I started coming here as snowbirds twelve years ago. He was a college professor at the University of Wyoming teaching economics. We vacationed in Arizona several times before moving here. Once Charles could teach online, we started coming here in the winter for three to four months. When he retired, we moved here full time. Unfortunately, Charles passed away two years ago. I stayed because all my friends are here and there are things to keep me busy. But I miss my Charles. This club has been very supportive of me. I think you will like our group."

"Sharon was one of the founding members of our book club," Linda advised.

"Impressive," replied Emily.

"My name is Judy Kinderman," announced Judy. "My husband and I are snowbirds. We split our time equally between here and Washington. Once it gets too hot in Arizona, we retreat to Washington for the summer months. My husband is a surgeon licensed in both states. That allows us to travel back and forth. I love reading crime novels and mysteries. This club focuses on those types of books. The women here support each other, which has made it easier to get through some tough times."

"How long have you been a snowbird?" asked Emily.

"This is our fifth winter," replied Judy.

"We've all shared our age, Judy," reminded Linda.

"Oh, yeah. I'm sixty-four."

"You don't look sixty-four," said Emily.

"It's her long blond hair," stated Sharon.

"Too bad her husband doesn't appreciate her more," said Katy.

"Katy!" snapped Linda.

"What? Everyone knows," said Katy.

Emily was looking around the room. Several members looked uncomfortable.

"It's okay. She would hear it eventually," sighed Judy. "My husband cheated on me. We're trying to work things out."

"I'm surprised to hear that," replied Emily. "You're a beautiful woman."

Judy smiled.

"Let's move on," said Linda. "Emily, it's your turn to tell us a little about yourself."

"Well, I'm sixty-six years old. I moved to Surprise three years ago from California."

"Ah, another foreigner," laughed Katy.

"Yeah, I get that a lot," replied Emily. "I understand. My husband, well, my ex-husband and I purchased a home here in Cactus View two years ago. After his accident, I thought about moving back to California. As luck would have it, I met Bill, who helped me through my grief. So, I'm still here. When I heard about your book club and the books you generally read, I decided to join. I love good crime mysteries, both fictional and true."

"You've come to the right club," said Linda.

"Do you have any particular authors you like?" asked Emily.

"Many of the authors I'm sure you know," answered Linda. "Authors like Ann Cleeves, James Patterson, David Baldacci, Lee Child."

"I really liked Along Came a Spider by Patterson. Have you read that one yet?" asked Emily.

"We have," said Linda.

"I think I will fit right in with this book club."

"I'm sure you will," agreed Linda. "Members are encouraged to suggest books to the group. After discussion, we all vote on which book to select. I will email you a list of the books we've read so that you know not to suggest those on the list."

"Thank you," replied Emily. "I'm not sure I can read two books a month. I might have to skim them."

"No, we only read one book a month, and sometimes we skip a month, especially in the summer. Our second meeting of each month is just social. Sometimes we will discuss high-profile crimes that are in the news. We're kind of like crime junkies, and we enjoy getting together."

"I see," replied Emily. "Sounds like fun."

Chapter 2

After the club members had finished discussing John Grisham's novel "The Reckoning," the conversation drifted into the happenings of their personal lives and the surrounding community. The Cactus View Book Club was as much about socializing as it was about books. Several members refilled wine glasses and sampled the snacks from the kitchen counter.

Katy Cullen drifted over to the newest member, Emily Settlemire. "Judy is having a tough time," Katy whispered.

"You mean about the affair?" asked Emily.

"Yes."

"That's sad. Judy is such a beautiful woman, and she seems nice enough."

"I've met her husband, and he comes across as a jackass if you ask me."

"Judy said they were trying to work things out," Emily reminded her.

"She tries to hide it, but I believe he is having another affair."

"Has Judy told you that?" asked Emily.

"You can see the signs. Judy has gotten more sullen over the last couple of weeks. She mentioned something about him not being able to control himself."

"Well, there's a simple fix to that. She should kick his ass out."

"Judy won't do that," insisted Katy.

"Why not?"

"She needs the money. She was a stay-at-home mom for most of their marriage. When she finally found a job, it was in retail. I believe she worked at Kohl's."

"And her husband is a surgeon," replied Emily. "They must have a lot of money. She is entitled to at least half of it."

"Well, Judy worries he would fight her and tie up the money for years. She's also afraid he would get the main house in Washington because that's where his primary practice is. That would leave her the house in Cactus View. She's not sure she would enjoy living here full time."

"If Judy needs advice on getting out of an awful marriage, send her to me," said Emily.

"What can you do?" asked Katy.

Before Emily could answer, Linda Riggs walked over. "We are delighted to have you in our club, Emily."

"Thank you."

"I don't want to pry, but you said your ex-husband had an accident a couple of years ago. Excuse me if I didn't understand, but it sounded like he might have passed away."

"He did," responded Emily. "And it happened just this last September. Fred fell while hiking in the White Tank Mountains. It was horrible."

"I'm so sorry," said Linda. "When you said ex-husband, I thought maybe you were now divorced."

"Why do you call him your ex-husband?" asked Katy.

"I don't know. Fred is dead now, so he's no longer my husband, right?"

Maritza Perez interrupted the conversation. She had a bottle of red wine in her right hand and white wine in her left. "Anyone need a fill-up?"

"White for me," said Emily.

"And I know you two like red," Maritza nodded to Katy and Linda. She then filled each of their glasses.

"Thank you, Maritza," said Linda.

"The last few months must have been hard on you," said Katy.

Emily didn't respond.

"Are you living alone now?"

"No," replied Emily. "I'm living with Bill, the friend who helped me get through the trauma of losing Fred."

"Oh," said Katy with raised eyebrows. "How did you meet this Bill fellow?"

"I got to know him from playing pickleball," said Emily.

"We're happy you're doing well," said Linda.

Katy walked over to Judy Kinderman and Sharon Jansen. "Did you know Emily's husband died in September while hiking in White Tank Park?"

Both women shook their heads no.

"And now she's living with the man who helped her in her grief, whatever that means."

"So what, Katy?" responded Sharon, the eldest and some thought the wisest of the group. "It's good she had a friend to help her. And she's too young to live the rest of her life alone."

"You live alone," said Katy.

"I'm seventy-seven and set in my ways. I had a great husband for forty-eight years, and I am very content with my life."

"If something happened to Jerry, moving in with someone else wouldn't even cross my mind," said Katy.

"People react differently," insisted Sharon. "At least she's happy. She could be miserable like Mary."

"Mary is being stubborn," said Katy. "She hasn't even been here for two years. This book club is the only thing she does. Mary could be happy if she wanted to be."

"You don't know the entire story, Katy," replied Judy. "Mary's husband abuses her."

"What? How?"

"He physically abuses her. I've told her to leave him, but she is too frightened."

"She told you this?" asked Katy.

"Once she found out about my cheating husband, she confided in me. You can't spread this around. I only told you so you would understand why she is so unhappy here."

"I didn't know that," sighed Katy.

"Okay, ladies. We need to wrap things up," announced Linda. "I promised Ray I would have us out of here by eight o'clock. He should be home soon."

Everyone helped pick up the food, wine bottles, and dishes. Once the house was back in order, everyone thanked Linda for hosting the book club meeting and sauntered out the door, chatting as they left.

Ray Riggs, Linda's husband, returned home at 8:15 p.m. "How did your book club go tonight?"

"It was interesting. We had a new member tonight. Her name is Emily Settlemire. She is a retired nurse who recently lost her husband in a hiking accident at the White Tank Mountain Park."

"What kind of accident?" asked Ray.

"She said he fell off the mountain while hiking."

"You know, I seem to remember hearing about a man falling off a steep cliff in Willow Canyon a few months ago," said Ray.

"Yeah, she said her husband died in September."

"Hmmm," grunted Ray. "Do you know his name?"

"Fred Settlemire."

"Fred Settlemire? I'll search online in the morning. There should be something I can find about it."

"Katy was a bit obnoxious about it."

"Katy obnoxious? That's hard to believe."

Linda laughed. "She also mentioned Judy's husband had cheated on her. I didn't think that was appropriate."

"It sounds like Katy. How is Judy doing?"

"I'm not sure," answered Linda. "She seemed less talkative than usual tonight."

"I thought things had gotten better."

"Me too. I will call her later this week to see how things are going. Other than that, things went well. I think Emily will fit right in."

Chapter 3

The next day, Thursday, thirty-three-year-old Maricopa County Detective Lou Begay was at his desk reviewing the reports on the death of Fred Levine. Levine had died three and a half months prior in a fall while hiking the Willow Canyon Trail in the White Tank Mountain Park just west of Surprise. Begay had doubts about whether the fall was accidental.

Fred Levine and his wife, Emily Levine, had been hiking the trail late afternoon on a Monday in September. As Emily reported, they were alone on the trail when Fred slipped or tripped on a rock, falling off the side of the trail into a steep canyon. He fell approximately eighty feet, coming to rest against some boulders near the bottom of the canyon. His injuries included several broken bones and a severe head wound. The coroner determined it was the head wound that killed him. The only witness to the accident was Emily Levine.

Several factors created doubt in Begay's mind. One, the couple was hiking on a day of the week and at a time when most people would not be on that difficult trail. Second, he knew Emily had moved in with another man, Bill Hutchins, only six weeks after her husband's death. He also knew Fred Levine had owned a chain of popular restaurants in California. He sold the restaurants prior to moving to Arizona for a whopping 8.5 million dollars. Emily was the sole benefactor in his will.

Finally, the assessment of Surprise Detective Dan Baxter concerned him the most. Baxter was a forty-three-year-old detective with twenty-one years of police experience, the last twelve as a detective. One of his specialties was in forestry and desert forensics. Baxter had assisted Begay in processing the scene of the accident. It was Baxter's opinion that Fred Levine was likely pushed over the canyon's edge. He based his opinion on examining the body's trajectory as it fell. Baxter noted the lack of soil disturbance near the edge of the trail. Second, the first evidence of impact on the side of the canyon was approximately twenty feet down the slope and ten feet out from the edge of the trail. Forensic analysis of the disturbance at the impact point found traces of skin cells and blood belonging to Levine. Baxter hypothesized Levine was pushed from the side of the trail with enough force to propel him away from the trail's edge. Another theory was that Levine was running as he went over the edge, propelling his body forward.

Begay picked up the phone and called Baxter at the Surprise Police Department.

"Detective Baxter speaking."

"Dan, It's Lou. Are you busy right now?"

"Not really."

"I'd like to review Fred Levine's death again. I have some additional information to share. Are you available for lunch? I'll buy."

"Uh, yeah, I can do that. You like Richi's Diner, correct?"

"Sure do."

"I'll meet you there in thirty minutes."

"See you then," agreed Begay.

Richi's Diner is a small restaurant in Surprise serving breakfast, lunch, and dinner. It is a favorite of the locals, especially the retired locals. The food is good, reasonably priced, and the staff is friendly.

Begay arrived at 11:45 a.m.. Baxter was already seated in a corner booth when he saw his Native American friend and detective approach. "Hi Lou," said Baxter.

Begay nodded. "Thanks for meeting with me."

"Sure. What's up?"

Just then, a young, dark-haired waitress walked up to ask them what they wanted to eat.

"The Philly Cheesesteak and a coffee for me," responded Begay.

"And I'll do the grilled cheese sandwich with bacon," said Baxter. "And an iced tea."

After the waitress left, Baxter looked at Begay. "Now, what's on your mind?"

"I've been going over the death of Fred Levine, and I have some new information I'd like to share."

"Sure, go ahead."

"Shortly after Levine's death, his widowed wife Emily changed her last name back to her maiden name, Settlemire. And get this, she inherited his eight million-dollar fortune."

"That could certainly be considered a motive," agreed Baxter.

"That's not all. I've discovered that six weeks after Fred's death, Emily moved into the home of family friend Bill Hutchins."

"Now that's interesting. Does Bill Hutchins also live in Cactus View?"

"He does. Bill Hutchins was a pickleball buddy of Fred's. He's also a retired fire captain. He retired from the Mesa Fire Department last June, then moved to Cactus View."

"Sounds to me like he might have been a friend of Emily's as well," responded Baxter.

"Yes. My sources have said Bill and Emily seemed overly friendly at times. Some were not surprised when Emily moved in with him."

"Based on this conversation, I'm guessing you think Emily killed Fred by pushing him off the mountain."

"You said the evidence indicated he may have been pushed."

"It's possible he could have been running and tripped, which may have propelled him over the side."

"Emily said nothing about him running. In her statement, Emily said she was walking in front of Fred when she heard him yell. As she turned around, she saw him falling down the mountainside."

"Had that happened," said Baxter, "there should have been some disturbance in the dirt and rocks at the trail's edge. I couldn't find any."

"Put it all together, and I believe Emily killed her husband for the money and to live with her secret lover," said Begay.

"I'm not sure you have enough to arrest her, let alone convince a jury. I could not confidently testify that Fred did not simply fall off the trail," said Baxter.

"But you don't believe that," said Begay.

"Here's what I struggle with," explained Baxter. "I don't know if Emily Levine is strong enough to push her husband into the air over the edge of that trail. The first evidence of impact is twenty feet below the edge."

Begay leaned back in the booth. "I hadn't thought of that."

"Fred Levine was about six-two and stocky. It would have taken someone stronger than Emily to shove him that hard."

"Yes, but being that large, if he had just lost his balance and fell, wouldn't he have tumbled down the mountainside from the edge of the trail?" asked Begay.

"Yes. And there should have been evidence of that long before twenty feet. That's what makes this such a mystery."

The waitress returned with their food and drinks. "Thank you," said Begay.

"We may not be solving anything today, but this food sure looks good," said Baxter.

Begay nodded as he bit into his juicy Philly Cheesesteak.

"I have an unrelated question," said Baxter.

"Yeah? What is it?"

"Is Begay your original Native American last name?"

"It was my father's surname. It translates to His Son. However, the original family name was Dancing Waters."

"Why was it changed?"

"Many Native Americans were forced to change their names by the government in the late eighteen and early nineteen hundreds. It was supposed to help us conform and assimilate into the new American way of life."

"Now that you say it, I remember reading that somewhere."

"Getting back to the case, here's a thought," said Begay. "What if there was someone else with them on the trail?"

"Was anyone else around when the police arrived?"

"No. But it was about an hour before the police could get to the location. Emily was the only one there. But someone could have been with them earlier."

"You might be reaching," said Baxter.

"I'm brainstorming. Maybe Bill Hutchins and Emily planned the whole thing. Maybe Hutchins was waiting for them on the trail."

"I suppose anything is possible, but you don't have any evidence of that."

"Hutchins is strong enough to shove Levine off the mountain, which would support your findings."

"If Hutchins was there, where was he when the police arrived?" asked Baxter.

"Maybe he had time to get off the mountain before their arrival."

"Even if you're right, it will be hard to prove. But I have to admit, the circumstances are very suspicious. If you need any help, let me know."

"Thank you, Dan. I think I'll put some more pressure on Emily. The first couple of times we talked, I wasn't aware of her relationship with Bill. We'll see how she handles some tough questions."

"Let me know if I can help," said Baxter.

After finishing their meals, Begay grabbed the check.

"I can pay my own way," insisted Baxter.

"Nope. I said I would buy if you met with me, and I appreciate your help."

"Alright. Well, thank you. Good luck with your investigation."

Chapter 4

Two days after the book club meeting, Mary Hipple and Emily Settlemire met for coffee at the Casa Café. The café was a local deli-style restaurant in the Cactus View Community Center. Many residents used the café as a meeting place, while others enjoyed having lunch there. It reminded Mary of an upscale courtyard at a vacation villa. Mary ordered a black coffee while Emily selected a coffee mocha. They sat at an outside patio table overlooking a small pond with Koi happily swimming around. A large blue table umbrella provided shade from the morning sun. Mary noticed Emily neatly dressed in a matching red outfit and black dress shoes. To Mary, Emily had overdressed for coffee.

"Thank you for asking me to coffee," said Mary. "I was a bit surprised."

"How so?" asked Emily.

"I didn't think we had much in common."

"Well, I got the sense you aren't happy in your marriage." Mary looked down at her coffee.

"By your body language, you're confirming my suspicion. I know how it feels, Mary. I'm someone you can talk to."

"I hardly know you," responded Mary.

"No, but I'm someone who struggled in a marriage, so I know how it can feel hopeless sometimes. I just wanted to reach out and let you know you're not alone."

"You were physically abused?" asked Mary.

"No, but I was not happy with my marriage."

"What was wrong with it?"

"Fred worked many hours and many years running his restaurants. When he came home late, he was usually tired or in a foul mood. I felt lonely. Once we moved to Cactus View, I thought things would change. But he got involved in so many activities nothing changed. He was happier, but I wasn't."

Mary cocked her head and frowned. "Didn't your husband recently pass away?"

"Yes. It was a terrible accident. We were hiking in White Tank Park when he slipped and fell down the mountainside."

"I'm sorry," said Mary. "But it sounds like you are happy he had an accident and died."

"No, I'm not happy about that. But I'm happy to be with someone who gives me the support and love I need. Bill does that for me."

"When did your husband have his accident?"

"Late last September. The twenty-seventh, to be exact."

"Three months ago?" Mary asked in astonishment.

"That's right."

"I thought it was two years ago. And you're already living with another man?"

"Bill was very comforting after Fred's death. I felt like it was meant to be. The important thing is that I'm happy now."

"I wish I could say that," replied Mary.

"You could be," said Emily.

Mary smirked. "I could never leave Eric. He wouldn't allow it."

"He doesn't have to allow it, Mary. You can take control of your own life. I take it from your question earlier that Eric has abused you. Am I right?"

Mary only looked down at the table.

"It's fairly obvious, Mary. How does he abuse you?"

"He yells at me for stupid things."

Emily saw a tear in Mary's right eye. "That's not all, is it? If you talk about it, you will feel better."

Mary reached into her pocket to pull out a Kleenex. She blew her nose, then looked up at Emily. "He sometimes hits me."

"Then why in hell haven't you left him, Mary?"

"I can't."

"Why not? Women leave their husbands all the time!"

Mary spoke softly. "You don't understand. He told me if I ever left him, I would get nothing. Most of his money is held in overseas accounts. Even if the court awarded me half of our money, I couldn't collect it."

"I'm sure he has a pension. You could get half of that. And then, if you sell your home, you would get half of that. Living with an abuser is not worth it."

"He managed a large construction company. He put his money into foreign annuities and investments. That is where we get our money. Only he has access to that," explained Mary.

"What about the house? It must be worth three-quarters of a million dollars."

"He's covered all the bases to make sure I never leave. You won't believe it if I tell you."

"Try me," said Emily.

"Eric's younger brother still lives in Minnesota. He is fifty-eight years old. Eric funneled the money to his brother, who then purchased the house we are living in. Eric's brother is an attorney, and he set up the whole deal. We only pay his brother a dollar a month to live there. I have no standing to the house."

Emily was shocked. "I don't see how that is possible."

"That's what he did. I can live in the house if Eric dies before me, but I won't own the house."

"What will you do for money?"

"Eric's brother, the attorney, will provide a monthly sum to live on so long as I never leave Eric while he is alive."

"Damn, I thought I had it bad," replied Emily.

There was silence for several seconds before Emily spoke up. "You don't have to live like this anymore, Mary."

"I have no choice, Emily."

"You always have a choice."

Mary was a bit irritated. "Okay, what choice do I have?"

"Well, you said once your husband dies, you will get to live in the house and receive money to live on. You would then be free to live as you want, do what you want, and love who you want."

Mary sighed. "Eric is still plenty healthy. I will probably die before he does."

"There are ways to change that," suggested Emily.

"What do you mean by that?"

"What if Eric happened to die before you?"

"There's a slim chance of that. He's in great shape. Look at me. I'm an overweight gray-haired woman who gets minimal exercise. It's probably why he doesn't love me anymore."

Emily lowered her voice. "But it could be arranged for him to die sooner, with no one knowing how. It can all look very natural or accidental."

Mary shifted in her chair. "What are you saying, Emily?"

"Mary, there are ways to create a death that is very natural or accidental. If that were to happen to your husband, you would be a free woman. Does he have life insurance?"

Mary's head was swirling with thoughts. "Uh, yes, he does. I forgot about that."

"Are you the beneficiary?"

"Believe it or not, I am. We got it when the kids were younger, so he wanted me to have the money for them. At least he cared about their future."

"How much is it for?"

"Two million dollars."

"Girl, you have nothing to worry about. All we need to do is get Eric to die."

"Emily, I'm not comfortable with you talking like that. It sounds like you are suggesting murder!"

"Lots of deaths are accidental, Mary. Or, sometimes, a person gets sick and dies. Both are very natural deaths. And then there's always suicide."

"Are you suggesting I should wish he gets hit by a car or commits suicide?"

"If you want. But wishing rarely works. I can see you're not quite ready to explore this option, but I want you to consider our conversation. If you decide you want to improve your lot in life, we can talk some more about it. It's not as hard or messy as you might think to assist someone into the world beyond."

"I.... I don't know what to say."

"You don't have to say anything right now, Mary. Just give our conversation a lot of thought."

Mary walked from the café to where her bright green electric Yamaha golf cart was parked. She slid behind the steering wheel and sat thinking about what Emily had said. She felt like she had just played a role in a sinister murder plot. Mary knew Judy Kinderman was also having marital problems. Judy's husband, Jack, had cheated on her in the past, and Judy suspected he was doing it again. Mary pulled out her cell phone and called Judy.

"Hello," answered Judy.

"Are you busy right now?"

"Not really. Why?"

"I'd like to come over to talk with you a bit. I had the strangest conversation with the new gal, Emily Settlemire. I need to tell you about it."

"Sure, come on over," said Judy.

"I'll be there in a few minutes," said Mary.

Mary started up her golf cart and maneuvered her way through the winding streets to Judy's beige stucco home. The giant, three-armed Saguaro Cactus in the front yard was an easy landmark to remember. Judy must have been looking out for Mary as she opened the front door when Mary approached.

"What a nice day for January," commented Judy. "It's supposed to hit seventy-one degrees today. Come on in."

Judy led Mary to the living room. Mary sat on the brown leather couch while Judy sat in the leather chair perpendicular to the sofa. "Would you like something to drink?" asked Judy.

"No, thank you. I've just had a large cup of coffee."

"Well then, tell me about your strange conversation."

"I'm not sure how to start. Uh, Emily wanted to talk to me about Eric."

"What about?"

"You're aware of the issues Eric and I have had."

"Yes. I know he's abusive."

"That's what Emily wanted to talk about. She tried to convince me I would be better off leaving Eric. She even insinuated there were ways to get rid of Eric so I could get the insurance money."

"Are you thinking of divorcing him?"

"I will only get the insurance money if Eric dies."

"Wouldn't you get half of everything in a divorce?" asked Judy.

"Not without a long, drawn-out fight. And maybe not even then. Eric has hidden the money in overseas accounts. And our house is in his brother's name."

"I see," said Judy.

"But if he dies, I would get two million from a life insurance policy."

"He seems healthy right now," said Judy.

"Yes. But Emily suggested there were ways to make a death look accidental."

Judy leaned in closer. "Is she talking about murder?"

"I'm not sure, but that was the impression I got. Setting someone up to die would be murder, right?"

"Well, yeah. And it could put you in prison, Mary."

"Judy, I sometimes feel like I'm already in prison. I know Jack's cheating has been very hard on you, so that's why I came to talk to you. If anyone can provide perspective, it would be you."

"Perspective on what? Getting divorced or killing my husband?"

"Emily lost her husband and is now happy living with another man."

"Yes, but that was an accident a couple of years ago."

"That's what I thought, too," continued Mary. "His accident occurred in late September, and she is already living with another man."

"This past September?"

"Yes."

"Wow, I didn't know it had only been a little over three months. Emily moves quickly."

"Yeah, and I'm not sure it was an accident," replied Mary.

"You think Emily killed her husband?"

"She called it an accident, but the way she talked to me, it was like she was encouraging me to find a way for Eric to die. Kind of like in an accident."

"That's a dangerous game, Mary."

"Believe me, I know. But I'm very unhappy with my situation. I came to talk with you because I know you're just as unhappy. I suspect Jack is cheating on you again. Am I right?"

Judy put her face in her hands, rubbing her temples. Her blond hair fell forward over her hands. "Is it that obvious?"

"I've suspected for a while now. You haven't been yourself lately, and you look uncomfortable whenever you are with Jack."

"Yes, I found out about it just before Thanksgiving. Whatever I provide him, it isn't enough. I wish I knew what was wrong with me."

"There is nothing wrong with you, Judy. Jack is the one with the problem. You still look young, slender, and your blond hair hides your age. You don't look like most sixty-four-year-old women."

"Apparently, I'm not good enough for Jack. He's always around so many young women nurses at the hospitals. He has a charisma about him."

"Why don't you divorce him?" asked Mary.

"I like the lifestyle. Jack makes good money, and we have these wonderful houses in Washington and Arizona. I'm not ready to give all that up."

"I understand the feeling."

"Tell me, Mary, is Eric still abusive?"

Mary looked into Judy's eyes, then looked down to hide the tears forming. She took a deep breath. "Sometimes, yes." Mary then cried openly.

Judy moved from her chair to sit next to Mary on the couch. She put her left arm around Mary's shoulders. "Have you ever considered calling the police?"

"I did once in Minnesota," sobbed Mary. "He was arrested but released shortly after. He had to do some probation time and counseling."

"Did he ever hit you again after that?"

"He was furious after I called the police, but he convinced his probation officer he had changed. Well, that was all an act. Shortly after his probation ended, he took me out to dinner. He even had me hire a babysitter so that we could be alone. But it wasn't just for dinner. He's like Jekyll and Hyde. After having a nice dinner, he took me to one of his extensive construction projects. I think it was an office building of some sort. Eric said he wanted to show me his new project. Once we were out of the car, his entire personality changed. He brings me to the edge of this big concrete hole in the ground, then grabs me by the back of my neck. And I'll never forget this. He pushes my head down so that I'm looking into the hole. He then says, in a voice I'll never forget, if you ever call the police on me again, I will bury you so deep in concrete no one will ever find you. Do we have an understanding? Judy, I was so frightened I was shaking. Of course, I said yes. He then took me home and forced me to have rough sex with him. I cried the whole time he was on me. I'll never call the police again."

Judy was horrified at what Mary had told her. "I'm so sorry, Mary."

"Now you know what I am up against," said Mary.

"Does he still physically hit you?"

"Most of the time, he just treats me poorly, screams at me and denies me things when he is angry. But occasionally, he will still hit me."

"I certainly have a better understanding of your situation. There must be something we can do."

"I think that's what Emily was trying to tell me," said Mary.

"I will admit your circumstances are not good, but murder doesn't seem to be the right way to solve this."

"What if it's just an accident?"

"How would you create an accident?"

"I don't know. But I had the impression from Emily that she would know how to create one."

"I'm uncomfortable with where this is going. Maybe we should stop talking about it."

"Well, thank you for taking the time to talk with me," said Mary.

"It felt good to share our misery," replied Judy. "Talking is always good for the soul. I'll give your situation some more thought, and maybe I can give you some ideas on how to get out of this marriage without going to prison."

"I think I've thought of most of them, but I'll listen to whatever you come up with."

"Goodbye, Mary. I'll see you later."

Mary climbed into her golf cart and checked her watch. It was almost 2:00 p.m. *I hope Eric's not home yet*, thought Mary.

By the time she arrived home, it was 2:15 p.m.. Eric's silver Corvette was parked in the driveway. Mary walked into the house and was immediately confronted by Eric.

"Where the hell have you been?" demanded an angry Eric.

"I was visiting a couple of friends and lost track of time. I'm sorry."

"You know my golfing buddies are coming for cards today at four o'clock. You were supposed to have the house cleaned and ready to go. Did you get the beer I asked you to pick up?"

"Oh, god, I forgot. I'm so sorry, Eric. I'll go get it now."

"No, I'll go get the beer. You get this house cleaned and start on the food. I swear, Mary, sometimes you're no smarter than a snail."

After Eric walked out the door, Mary gently cried as she picked up the living room.

Chapter 5

The following Monday, Linda Riggs, Maritza Perez, and Katy Cullen met for their bi-weekly luncheon. On this day, they were meeting at Panera's on Bell Road. After each had ordered their lunch, Linda asked Maritza and Katy what they thought of the new book club member.

"I'm not sure about her," said Katy.

"She seemed nice enough to me," countered Maritza. "What aren't you sure about?"

"She seemed a bit snooty to me," replied Katy, "with her highlighted light brown hair and fancy dress."

"Come on, Katy," said Linda. "We all try to look our best. She probably didn't know to dress casually."

"Well, you know her husband died, right?" said Katy.

"Yes, she told us that. It was a hiking accident."

"Yeah, and then she moved in with another man," said Katy. "Don't you find that strange?"

"A little bit, but everyone is different."

"I think I would have been traumatized for a long time if I lost Ricardo. I'm not sure I could ever date again," said Maritza.

"Well, I talked to Judy over the weekend," continued Katy. "She told me Emily tried to talk Mary into leaving her husband. She hardly knows Mary, and she's already butting into her business."

"Maybe Mary needed to hear that," replied Linda.

"Judy then told me Emily suggested getting rid of Mary's husband by an accident or something."

"Oh, come on. That can't be true," replied Linda. "Mary has been out of sorts lately. She must have misunderstood the conversation."

"I can't answer that," said Katy. "But I also find it strange when a woman immediately moves in with another man shortly after her husband has a terrible accident."

"It does seem awfully soon," agreed Linda.

"I have a strange feeling about Emily," continued Katy. "With her highlighted light brown hair, stylish glasses, well-endowed figure and fancy clothes, it's no wonder she has men after her."

"I'm not sure any of that is relevant," replied Maritza. "We all try to look our best. It doesn't mean she's looking for men."

"I don't think Mary tries to look her best," said Katy.

"Really, Katy?" asked Linda. "That's kind of mean."

"I'm just saying she could look better if she wanted to."

"Maybe she doesn't want to," said Maritza. "Her marriage sucks. Would you want to look good for that man?"

"How good was Emily's marriage before her husband's death?" asked Katy.

"I don't know, but it sounded like she needed help with the grieving process," said Linda.

"And she is so distraught that she moves in with this Bill character within weeks?" asks Katy.

Several seconds of silence passed. "People respond to grief differently," suggested Linda. "Maybe she just needed a shoulder to cry on."

"And a man to sleep with," added Katy.

"You are making many assumptions," said Linda. "Maybe we need to discuss how to help Mary. She seems to be the one that needs our support right now."

"Well, if we help her dump Eric, she can move back to Minnesota to help her mom and be around her children," said Katy.

"All she has to do is get a divorce," said Maritza.

"Apparently," said Katy, "Eric has the money tied up in a way that prevents Mary from getting any of it in a divorce. Furthermore, they don't own their own house. Eric's brother owns the house. The only thing Mary will get is a two-million-dollar life insurance payment should Eric die."

"That's crazy," said Linda.

Katy turned to Maritza. "Your husband Ricardo is an attorney, right?"

"Yes."

"Then he should be able to help Mary."

"He's not a divorce lawyer, but I can ask him what he thinks."

"I'm not sure we should even get involved," said Linda. "Eric has a temper, and we could make things worse for Mary."

"It won't hurt just to ask Ricardo's opinion," said Katy.

"It will be okay," said Maritza. "Ricardo won't get involved, but he'll tell her what he thinks. He's going to need more detailed information. Will Mary talk to him?"

"I don't know," replied Katy.

Later that day, Linda's husband Ray returned home from his workout at the Cactus View Recreation Center.

"How was your luncheon?"

"It was interesting, to say the least," replied Linda. "Katy told us that our new club member, Emily, was trying to talk Mary into getting rid of her husband."

"She should have divorced him a long time ago," replied Ray.

"Katy made it sound like Emily suggested an accident of some sort."

"An accident?"

"Yeah, that's what we thought. From what Katy said, Eric has all the money tied up somewhere, and the house they live in is owned by his brother. But there is a two-million-dollar insurance policy that would go to Mary should Eric die."

Ray was silent. "What are you thinking?" asked Linda.

"Our conversation the other night led me to do some research into the death of Emily's husband. I searched for the name Settlemire, and nothing came up. So, I searched for any hiking deaths at White Tank Mountain. The only death in the last ten years was Fred Levine back in September. He fell off a cliff while hiking."

"Yes, that's Emily's deceased husband. It happened just over three months ago."

"I thought Emily's last name was Settlemire?"

"Maybe she never took his name."

"Hmmm. I don't believe the police have closed the case yet."

"What do you mean?"

"From the accounts I read online, it sounds like the investigation hasn't been closed yet."

"Do the police believe it was something other than an accident?"

"I can't tell from the articles, but whenever a case remains open, that indicates the police have some questions about the facts. And after what you just told me, I'm concerned."

"Well, Maritza is going to have her husband look into getting Mary out of her marriage with some money to live on."

"Is that what Mary wants?"

"I haven't asked her directly, but I can tell she is unhappy in her marriage."

"Be careful, Linda. You don't need to be involved in Mary's marital problems or in some scheme to get rid of her husband."

****

It was the last Wednesday in January when Surprise Detective Dan Baxter met with Maricopa County Detectives Lou Begay and Leland Ashford on the Willow Canyon Trail in the White Tank Mountain Regional Park. The detectives were casually dressed in blue jeans and windbreakers. They rode small ATVs up the trail with a load of three 80-pound sandbags. They stopped at the location where Fred Levine had fallen to his death.

"This is where Emily Levine told us Fred stumbled and fell over the edge into the canyon," said Begay as he pointed to the spot. When processing the scene, a stake had been driven into the mountainside to mark the location.

Detective Baxter used his binoculars to look down the mountainside. He then handed them to Detective Ashford.

"Look about twenty to twenty-five feet down to the jagged boulder that sort of looks like a turtle," said Baxter.

Ashford looked for several seconds. "Yes, I see it."

"That's where I found the first evidence of impact," said Baxter. "From there, I found evidence every five to ten feet of our victim rolling and bouncing down the mountain."

"The slope is not that steep right here," said Ashford. "I now understand why you think he may have been pushed."

"We will use these sandbags to see how they fall from the edge," said Begay. "We will try to simulate someone tripping over the ledge first. Leland, I'd like you to video the bag rolling down the slope."

"Got it."

"After that, we will use greater force to toss the bags away from the trail while videoing how they fall."

"I'm ready when you are," replied Ashford.

Baxter assisted Begay in carrying the first bag to the trail's edge. "Let's give it a slight push as though this bag lost its footing," said Baxter.

The detectives pushed the first bag over the edge and watched it tumble down. The bag rolled and tumbled, disrupting the soil and small rocks as it traveled down the mountain.

"Now look at the trail the bag left," said Baxter. "Can you see the disturbances in the soil?"

"No question," replied Begay.

"Okay, now we will toss the second bag over the edge, trying to simulate someone who may have been jogging and stumbled. How far out do you think we should toss it?" asked Baxter.

"Levine probably weighed one-ninety to two hundred pounds," said Begay. "Maybe five feet or so?"

"I agree," said Baxter. "See that small teddy bear cactus right there? Let's toss this bag right next to it."

Begay and Baxter each grabbed one end of the bag and swung it over the trail's edge. The bag first hit the ground just to the right of the cactus. It then tumbled down the mountain, much like the first bag did.

"We need to simulate someone pushing this last bag over the edge as though it was a person," said Baxter. "Leland, can you move that ATV close to the edge here?"

"Sure thing."

Once the ATV was in place, Baxter and Begay lifted the heavy bag up onto the seat of the ATV. They set the bag in a vertical position.

"This is obviously not an exact simulation," said Baxter. "We can't shove a human being over the edge. However, by placing this bag on the ATV, we can at least shove the bag from a higher level. This would be like someone being shoved in the back. The weight is different, so I must judge how much force to use."

Begay held one hand on the bag to keep it upright as Baxter positioned himself behind it. Baxter imagined himself coming up from behind someone and shoving them. He lowered his center of gravity for more lift as he approached the bag. As he hit the bag, he pushed it as hard as he could without falling over the ATV. The bag flew off the ATV and over the edge of the trail. It flew out approximately six feet before arcing downward, first striking a round boulder. It then continued to tumble another ten feet before lodging against some rocks. Baxter carefully climbed down the side while extending a tape measure.

"The first point of impact is twelve feet," announced Baxter. He then climbed his way back to the trail.

"What does it all mean?" asked Begay.

"Well, eighty-pound sandbags are not two-hundred-pound human beings. Having said that, at least we demonstrated that simply falling over the edge differs from being propelled over the edge."

"Do you believe foul play was involved?" asked Ashford.

"I don't believe this would convince a jury he was murdered," replied Baxter. "But we can convincingly say he did not simply trip over the edge or lose his balance while looking over the edge. Either someone pushed him over, or he committed suicide by running and jumping off the edge."

"Could Emily have pushed him?" asked Begay.

"Yes, of course. But I don't think she could have applied enough force to propel a two-hundred-pound man out that far. The first impact was twenty feet down."

"So I've got nothing but suspicion," replied Begay.

"Have you questioned Mrs. Levine again?"

"Not yet. And the name is now Settlemire."

"Ah, yes. I forgot. Have you talked to the new boyfriend?"

"Talking to both of them is next on my list. I wanted to get this test done first. I will use this data when I confront Emily."

"Talk to the first responding officer as well," suggested Baxter. "Find out if he saw anyone else on the trail as he was getting to the scene."

"Good idea. Thanks, Dan."

Chapter 6

It was 9:10 a.m. on February 2nd when Detective Begay rang the doorbell on Bill Hutchins' door. The day was unusually cool, with overcast skies. The average temperature for Surprise in February is seventy-one degrees. This day's high was only expected to hit sixty-two degrees with a northwest wind. Begay was wearing his navy-blue windbreaker.

Emily Settlemire was in the kitchen when she heard the doorbell ring. She was dressed but hadn't yet put on any makeup. Emily quickly brushed her fingers through her light brown hair while looking at her reflection in the microwave door. She then walked to the front door and opened it.

"Good morning, Emily," said Begay. "I'm Detective Begay with the Maricopa County Sheriff's Office."

"Ah, yes. I recognize you now. How can I help you?"

"I just have a few follow-up questions regarding your husband's death. May I come in?"

Emily opened the screen door. "Sure, come on in. Would you like to sit in the living room?"

"Why don't we sit at the dining table if that's okay?"

Emily walked to the oak table and sat down. Begay selected a chair directly across from Emily. He briefly glanced around the large room and could tell Hutchins had a lot of money. The dining area and living room were furnished with high-end furniture, and expensive artwork accented the rooms.

"Is Bill home this morning?" asked Begay.

"No. He's working out at the rec center. What can I answer for you, Detective?"

"Some questions have come up during our investigation of your husband's death, Mrs. Levine. I'm sorry, your name is now Settlemire, correct?"

"Yes."

"Did you use your husband's last name while he was alive?"

"Yes."

"How soon after Fred's death did you change your name?"

"I simply went back to using my maiden name."

"How soon?" pressed Begay.

"Gee, I don't know. Probably after about a month."

"How long were you married to Fred?"

"We were married for twenty-two years."

"Any children?"

"No. We were both in our forties when we married."

"Any previous marriage?"

Emily frowned. "What does this have to do with Fred's accident?"

"This is just background information we get on any investigation. Were you married before Fred?"

"Yes."

"Who were you married to before?"

"I don't understand your line of questioning, Detective."

"Look, the Sheriff demands that our investigation of any death is thorough, including background information on witnesses. Please, just help me complete my report."

"My first marriage was to Scott Ridley. I was only twenty years old. It only lasted four years."

"How did the marriage end?"

"We were too young. We just decided to split up."

"And was Fred your second marriage?" Begay could tell Emily did not like the question. "I can research it, Emily, but it would be easier if you answered my question."

"My second marriage was to Chuck Landowski. I married him when I was thirty-five."

"How did that marriage end?"

"Chuck got very ill, and he eventually died."

"I'm sorry to hear that," said Begay. "Do you know what he died from?"

"Some intestinal problems. Chuck had been sick for some time."

"What city was this in?"

"Riverside, California."

"How old were you when Chuck died?"

"I was forty-three."

"And when did you marry Fred?"

"When I was forty-four. Why is this so important now? Fred's death was an accident four months ago. I thought the investigation was over long ago."

"It's not over yet, Emily. We are simply creating a history so that we can close it out. This is routine stuff. Doing my math here, if Chuck died when you were forty-three, you got married to Fred soon after Chuck's death. Is that correct?"

"It was six months after Chuck's death."

"Thank you, Emily. Let's review Fred's accident again to ensure I have the facts correctly. Can you explain what happened one more time, please?"

Emily looked irritated. "As I've told you and others already, Fred and I were hiking the Willow Canyon Loop. I was walking in front of Fred. I didn't see what happened. All I heard was Fred cry out. I turned to see what was wrong and saw Fred tumbling down the canyon. I climbed down to help him, but it became too steep, and it looked like he was dead already. I was afraid I would fall if I continued."

"How far did you climb down the canyon?"

"Probably at least halfway to Fred."

"And then you climbed back out. Was it hard to climb back up?"

"Yes. I had to crawl out to avoid falling."

"Thank you, Emily. Now I will ask some questions my bosses are asking, so please forgive me."

"What questions?"

"When did you begin dating Bill Hutchins?"

Emily hesitated. "I didn't start seeing Bill until after Fred's death."

"How long after his death?"

"It was six weeks after Fred's death. Bill had been a friend and was there for me in my grieving. We developed a relationship. But you already know all this."

"No, it was six weeks after Fred's death that you moved in with Bill," Begay reminded her. "I asked when you started seeing him, as in dating."

For the first time, Begay detected some nervousness in Emily. He saw her swallow as she twirled her hair with her right hand.

"I guess we started a relationship about two weeks before I moved in."

"By your timeline, you were dating Bill only four weeks after Fred's accident."

Begay observed tears in Emily's eyes.

"I was in shock and an emotional mess," cried Emily. "Bill was a shoulder to cry on. Have you ever lost someone you loved?"

Begay ignored the question. "Some people have told me you were having an affair with Bill before Fred's death."

"Who said that?!" demanded Emily. "That is not true. I loved Fred."

Begay noted the quick change in Emily's demeanor from sadness to anger.

"How did you first meet Bill?"

"I like to keep myself in shape. I met Bill in the weight room at the rec center. He helped set me up with a program. He was a nice man."

"I thought you knew him from pickleball?" asked Begay.

"Fred knew him from pickleball, and I would sometimes play with them," said Emily.

"When was the first time you met Bill?"

"About a year ago."

"And is Bill retired?"

"Yes. Bill was a firefighter in Peoria for thirty years and retired as a captain. After retirement, he moved to Cactus View."

"Was Bill married at the time?"

"No. He was divorced years ago."

"Did Fred know about Bill?"

"Know about him? Bill was a friend to both of us."

"Did Fred know you were seeing Bill?"

"I never said that!" said Emily in a raised voice. "Don't put words in my mouth."

"You're telling me the first time you started seeing Bill as more than a friend was after Fred's death, correct?"

"Yes."

"Some people have said you and Bill were close before that," said Begay.

"They're wrong."

Begay sensed Emily was lying.

"Who else was with you and Fred on your hike?"

"What?"

"You just said Bill was a friend to both of you. I thought maybe he had gone on the hike as well."

"It was only Fred and I."

"We have evidence that Fred was pushed off the mountain. Did you push him off?"

"That's ridiculous!" shouted Emily.

"He did not just fall off the trail, Emily. He either jumped, or someone pushed him. Did you push him?"

"I absolutely did not push Fred."

"Did Bill push Fred off the mountain?"

Emily let out a big laugh, which sounded like a nervous laugh to Begay. "Now you are just being ridiculous," said Emily. "Fred and I were alone, and he accidentally tripped or slipped off the mountain. I think I've answered enough questions now."

"Yes, you have. Thank you for your time. I will need to talk to Bill as well. Here is my card. Please have him call me."

Emily didn't respond as Begay let himself out. However, Begay was pleased with the interview. In his assessment, Emily was lying. The most telling answers for Begay were Emily's answers to his last two questions. Her answer was definitive when asked if she had pushed Fred off the mountain. She stated, "I absolutely did not push Fred." However, when asked whether Bill had pushed Fred, Emily avoided answering. Her response was to laugh nervously, then reiterated that she and Fred were alone. But she avoided answering no. Avoiding direct answers is indicative of lying. Finally, Begay believed Emily had lied about climbing down the mountainside to help Fred. Emily's clothing and hands were clean at the scene. This would have been unlikely had she just climbed down and back up the side of the Canyon. Furthermore, Detective Baxter had not found evidence that someone had scrambled down or up the canyon slope. He didn't know how he would prove it, but he now believed Emily and Bill had killed Fred Levine.

After Detective Begay had left, Emily was pleased with her performance. In her mind, she answered all the detective's questions, providing no incriminating evidence. Emily tried to call Bill on his cell phone, but there was no answer. She would have to wait until he returned to tell him about the interview.

Once he returned to his office, Begay called Detective Baxter. "Hi, Lou. What's up?"

"I just got back from a follow-up interview with Emily Settlemire. As expected, she denied pushing Fred or that anyone else was with them on the hike. She also claimed to have tried to help Fred by climbing down the mountainside after he fell."

"As I recall from the photographs you showed me, it didn't look like Emily had just climbed down that slope," said Baxter.

"Yeah, she was lying. She got nervous when I questioned her about Bill. Emily was strong in denying she pushed Fred but didn't give me a direct answer when I asked if Bill had pushed him."

"We have no evidence Bill was even there," said Baxter.

"No, but if your analysis is correct, someone must have pushed Levine off that trail. Oh, and get this. Emily has been married twice before. One ended in divorce, and the second ended in her husband's death from an unknown illness. She then married Fred six months after the death of her second husband."

"Hmmm, that's interesting," said Baxter.

"Yeah, that's what I thought as well," agreed Begay.

Bill Hutchins returned to his home at 11:15 a.m.. Emily was waiting for him. "Why didn't you answer your phone?" asked Emily.

"I was working out, then took some time in the hot tub. What's wrong?"

"That county detective came by to ask me more questions about Fred," said Emily. "He started asking about us and wanted to know if you were on the hike."

"What did you tell him?"

"I told him Fred and I were alone. He then accused me of pushing Fred off the trail."

"He's just fishing for answers, Emily. The cops have no evidence of anything other than it being an accident. Stop worrying. Go fix yourself up, and I'll take you out for lunch at that new winery by Costco."

"Cooper's Hawk?" asked Emily.

"Yes, that's it."

"I'll be ready in a few minutes," said Emily.

After talking with her husband, Ricardo, Maritza Perez telephoned Linda Riggs.

"Hello, Maritza. What's up?"

"Ricardo did some checking with a divorce lawyer he knows, and the feedback was not encouraging," said Maritza. "To check into Eric Hipple's financial holdings, he would need either Mary's permission or a court order."

"I can ask Mary, but I think she is too fearful of Eric to grant permission. Who knows how Eric would react?"

"The other way is for Mary to file for divorce. Eric would then be required to provide his financials to the court."

"I'll let Mary know. Thank you for trying, Maritza."

Linda called Mary Hipple. "Hello," answered Mary.

"Mary, it's Linda. I just got off the phone with Maritza. She had her husband look into your husband's financial holdings. According to..."

"What?" interrupted Mary. "What are you talking about?"

"Katy told Maritza and I about your situation. We thought maybe Ricardo could check into your husband's finances to help you get a divorce."

"Why would you do that? If Eric finds out, my life will be hell. You had no right to do that without talking to me!"

"I'm sorry, Mary. You are right. We were just trying to help. Eric won't find out. No one else knows we even asked."

"I can take care of myself," said an angry Mary.

"I'm sorry. We are worried..."

Mary abruptly disconnected the call.

Linda then called Maritza. "Maritza, say nothing about Mary's situation and don't tell anyone we tried to get your husband to help."

"I won't. What happened?"

"I just got off the phone with Mary to tell her what your husband said. She didn't even let me finish. She was furious."

"Okay. I won't mention it."

Chapter 7

On February 3rd, Detective Begay called Bill Hutchins on his cell phone.

"Hello,"

"Mr. Hutchins, this is Detective Lou Begay. I want to discuss Fred Levine's accident with you. What time do you have available?"

"I've already answered police questions, Detective. I was not involved and have nothing more to say."

"Often, people think they have nothing that will help an investigation, but any information could be helpful."

"Detective, Emily was upset with your line of questioning yesterday. Fred's fall was an accident. We have nothing more to say. Goodbye."

"No luck," said Begay to Detective Ashford, seated nearby.

"Won't talk, eh?" asked Ashford.

"No. It only adds to my suspicion. I think Hutchins is involved, but I can't figure out how no one saw him or how he got on and off that damn trail."

"Maybe he was hiding somewhere."

"I thought of that, but where? And how did he get up there with no one seeing him?"

Ashford shook his head. "I don't know."

Begay picked up his phone and punched in the number to the Riverside, California Police Department. "Yes, this is Detective Lou Begay with Maricopa County in Arizona. Could you please transfer me to a detective in your homicide unit? Thank you."

After several seconds, Detective Tom Gomez answered the phone.

"Detective, this is Detective Lou Begay from Maricopa County, Arizona."

"Yes, what can I do for you?"

"I'm investigating a death that is likely a homicide. My suspect is a woman named Emily Settlemire. I suspect she killed her husband. Twenty-two years ago, she lived in Riverside and was married to Chuck Landowski. He apparently died from a sickness, but I'm wondering if there was more to it. Could you check your files to see if there was an investigation into his death?"

"That's a long time ago. I wasn't around then, but I'll look into it for you," answered Gomez.

The following day, Emily arranged lunch with Mary and Judy at the Rio Mirage on North Litchfield Road. Mary and Judy were already seated with their margaritas when Emily arrived. As usual, Emily looked overdressed for the casual lunch.

"I see you've already started," said Emily.

"It's the two-for-one special today," replied Judy.

"Then I guess I'll have to order two for myself."

Emily waved the waiter over. "I'll have the two margarita specials and another one for my friends to share."

"I'm good," said Mary.

Emily held up her hand. "You can handle another margarita, and I'm buying." Emily nodded at the waiter.

"Why did you want to meet for lunch?" asked Judy.

"You are two of my new book club friends. I'm trying to get to know the members. What better way than having lunch together where we can talk? Besides, I need some new friends."

"I'm sure you've made friends over the last two years," said Judy.

"Yes, but most of those were also Fred's friends. I need some new friends now. When I get together with them, they either want to talk about Fred or question me about living with Bill. I don't need that. I also know both of you could use some support."

Mary looked down.

"What kind of support?" asked Judy.

"I've gone through marital problems before, so I know what it's like. I loved Fred, but we had grown distant. And my second husband cheated on me, so I know what that is like."

"You've been married twice?" asked Judy.

"No. Three times."

"Three times? I might have given up by now."

"Marriage is hard, isn't that right, Mary?" asked Emily.

"You know what's going on with Eric and me," replied Mary.

The waiter approached with four margaritas and distributed them around the table. "What would you like to order today?"

"I'll take the chicken tostada lunch special," said Judy.

"And I'll have the fajita taco salad," replied Mary.

"Give me the mini chicken salad," said Emily. "I need to keep my figure."

Judy rolled her eyes.

"Oh, this will be all on one check to me," said Emily.

"You don't have to do that," said Judy.

"I want to. Just relax and enjoy our lunch together. I want to know more about how the two of you are coping."

"We're still on our first marriage," said Judy. "We should ask how you are coping. Three marriages and now living with another man. What's up with that?"

"It's simple. In my first marriage, we were both too young. We wanted different things in life. It was an amicable divorce. My second marriage lasted eight years. I found out Chuck was cheating on me, and then he died. And you already know about Fred."

Judy was a bit stunned. "Did you leave your second husband before he died?"

"No. Chuck died after I found out he was cheating. He developed some internal issues that eventually killed him."

"Were you going to leave him?"

"I was. But when Chuck got sick, I stuck it out until he died. That way, I got all the money in the relationship rather than just half if I divorced him."

"That seems diabolical," said Mary.

"It's called good financial planning," said Emily. "It's something I tried to talk to you about last week. Your situation is not good unless you do something about it."

The waiter returned with the food.

"Thank you," said Emily. "Three more rounds of margaritas, please."

Judy held up her hand. "No more for me."

"Come on, Judy. It's ladies' lunch and happy hour on me."

"I have to drive," responded Judy.

"We'll be here for some time, and I'll get you a ride if you need it. We all have to let loose sometimes."

Judy shook her head. "I can't drink that much. I'm already feeling buzzed, and I still have another one to drink."

"What about you, Mary? You up for a party lunch?" asked Emily.

"What the hell. With the way my marriage is, why not?"

"Make that just two more rounds," said Emily.

The waiter smiled and nodded.

"Now, let's get back to our marriage discussion," suggested Emily. "Where were we?"

"How are you so unlucky to have two husbands die on you?" asked Mary.

"I don't consider it unlucky when a cheating husband dies and leaves you a bunch of money."

"How can you be so callous about it?" asked Judy.

"Let me ask you this, Judy. Are you happy in your marriage right now?"

After several seconds, Judy said, "No."

"This isn't the first time Jack has cheated on you, is it?"

Judy shook her head no.

"He likes those flirty nurses too much, right?"

"Yeah. It's like Jack can't help himself."

Emily leaned toward the table. "How in the hell can you be casual about Jack's cheating?"

"I'm not casual about it!"

"Sure you are. How many times, Judy?"

"At least twice."

"Twice? You don't believe that, though, do you? I can see it in your body language. How many times? Three? Five?"

"Probably multiple times."

"Now you are being more honest. Margaritas are like truth serum. Drink up that third one, and we can have a genuine conversation."

Mary was watching the back-and-forth with excited nervousness. She finished her third margarita just as the waiter brought her and Emily two more.

Emily looked at Mary. "And what about you?"

Mary sat up. "What do you mean?"

"I mean, why are you still in a relationship that sucks? No one deserves to be abused."

"Uh, I told you my situation."

"Getting out of your marriage would not be worse than what you have now. It would help if you took control of your life back. You look like you don't even care anymore."

"What do you mean?"

"Look at how you dress. Jeans and T-shirts are not all that flattering. That short hairstyle does nothing for you. And you obviously don't work out. Am I right?"

Mary was taken aback.

Emily continued. "Probably the only sex you have is when that jackass husband of yours demands it. Am I right?"

Mary looked surprised. "How do you know so much?"

"I observe and pay attention to behavior. At the book club meeting, it was clear both of you were in unhappy marriages. I can help you."

"How did you know Eric demands sex?"

"I read the signs, and then when you explained how he controls everything, it was an assumption."

"I've never met anyone like you," said Judy.

The waiter walked up with two more margaritas for Emily and Mary.

"It's good these are the smaller ones," sighed Mary. "I'm not feeling any pain right now."

"Okay, so you know we have lousy marriages," said Judy. "But you make it sound like there are easy fixes. Not all of us want to change husbands every few years."

"I'll take that as a compliment," laughed Emily.

Judy could tell Emily was slightly intoxicated. "The husbands you didn't want all died," said Judy.

"Not all of them," Emily reminded her. "Just the last two."

"My mistake," said Judy. The margaritas gave Judy courage. "Last week, Mary told me about your conversation on getting rid of Eric. Exactly what were you proposing?"

The tequila was also working its magic on Emily. "Divorce the jerks. And if you don't want to do that, some diseases and accidents kill people all the time."

"See," said Mary. "That's how she was talking last week."

"Your solution is to create an accident or infect them with a disease?" asked Judy.

"Only if you don't want the consequences of a divorce and will take some risk for big rewards."

"Divorce isn't so bad," responded Judy.

"Why should you only get half of everything if your husband has been cheating on you for years? He's a surgeon, right?"

"Yeah."

"So, I'm sure his big-shot attorneys would create an issue for you in a divorce. I'm just saying divorce is not always the best option. In Mary's case, I think her husband would kill her rather than divorce her. Am I right, Mary?"

"He's already threatened to kill me."

"See?" said Emily.

Judy lowered her voice. "You're talking about murder."

Emily smiled, and her glazed eyes looked directly into Judy's. "It's not murder if no one knows it was murder."

Judy leaned toward Emily. "Did you kill Fred, Emily?"

Emily shook her head. "Fred fell off a mountain."

"What about your second husband?"

"He got sick and died."

"Then why are you trying to talk us into killing our husbands?"

"It's not murder if no one knows it was murder."

Mary picked up her last margarita and slurped it down.

"I think she's saying..."

"Yeah, I know what she's saying, Mary. So, Emily, how might Mary's husband have an accident?"

Emily was visibly intoxicated. "There are lots of accidents that could happen. Falling off a mountain, drowning, or getting hit by a car, to name a few."

"You're serious, aren't you?" asked Judy.

"Marriage can be hard," said Emily. "You bet I'm serious."

The margaritas had loosened Mary's inhibitions as well. "Hypothetically, how would you suggest I get rid of Eric?"

"There are lots of ways, honey. You have to be creative and have tight lips."

"Tight lips? What do you mean?" asked Mary.

"You can never tell anyone what you've done," said Emily.

The waiter came by to see if the ladies wanted any more drinks.

"No, we've had enough," said Judy. "The meal was delicious. Just bring us the check."

The waiter handed Judy the check.

"Give it to me," demanded Emily.

Judy handed Emily the check. "Thank you for lunch, Emily. It has been both interesting and enlightening."

"Yes, thank you," said Mary.

After Emily paid for the tab, Judy insisted on driving them back to Cactus View. "Neither of you is in any condition to drive."

Judy dropped Emily off first at Bill Hutchins' home.

"Thank you, ladies. It was fun. Let's plan coffee on Friday, and we can talk some more."

"We'll see," replied Judy.

Judy next stopped in front of Mary's home. Mary hesitated in getting out of the car.

"What do you think about our discussion today?" asked Mary.

"I don't know. What do you think?"

"I must admit, I like the idea of being rid of Eric," admitted Mary. "Emily made it sound easy to arrange an accident or illness. Not that I want to, but I don't know any other way out."

"It scares me to even think about it," said Judy.

"Will you be at book club on Wednesday?" asked Mary.

"Yes. I'll see you there."

Detective Begay's cell phone rang. He could see it was from the Riverside Police Department. "Hello," answered Begay.

"Hi, Detective Tom Gomez with the Riverside Police Department."

"Yes, thanks for calling me back, Tom. Were you able to find anything on Chuck Landowski's death?"

"We had nothing in our database or files on Landowski's death. However, I retrieved a death certificate from the county. Cause of death was liver failure."

"Nothing suspicious about the death?"

"Not from anything I found."

"No autopsy?" asked Begay.

"Not that I can find," said Gomez.

"Thank you for checking, Tom."

"Sure. Let me know if there is anything else I can do for you."

"I will, thanks."

Chapter 8

It was 6:00 p.m. the following Wednesday. Members arrived for the Cactus View Book Club carrying snacks and bottles of wine. Everyone except Maritza Perez was present for the gathering. Maritza and her husband Ricardo were attending a musical show at the community theater.

"Where is Maritza tonight?" asked Sharon Jansen, the group's eldest member.

"She's attending a show with her husband," replied Linda. "It's a Stevie Wonder show."

"Ah, I didn't care for him much," said Sharon.

"Stevie Wonder is playing here?" asked Emily.

"No," said Linda. "Someone who imitates Stevie Wonder."

"Of course. Well, I liked his music."

"Thank you for your feedback on this month's book," announced Linda. "Based on the feedback I received via email, our book for this month will be The Girl From Silent Lake by Leslie Wolfe."

"Good choice," said Katy. "I've already started it."

"Okay, tonight is casual night. No topic is off-limits. Grab some wine, some food, and relax," said Linda.

"I like the sound of that," smiled Emily as she filled a long-stem wine glass with Merlot.

Katy leaned in toward Sharon. "Can you believe how showy Emily dresses? It looks like she's going to a formal dinner."

"She looks great," replied Sharon. "I can't wear heels like that anymore."

The wine and conversation flowed freely. Members shared stories from the past two weeks, covering topics such as movies, friendships, and recent activities. Mary was pouring herself a glass of Chardonnay when Katy saddled up next to her.

"How are you doing, Mary?"

"I'm fine."

"Have you talked further with Emily about Eric?"

"How do you know about that?"

"Word gets around. I'm concerned about you."

"It's not your problem, Katy."

"You're a friend. I don't enjoy seeing you get abused."

"When have you ever seen that?"

"It's obvious when you two are together. Eric is very controlling. I see how he treats you. And I know you've shared your abuse with Emily."

"Huh?"

"And Judy certainly knows."

Mary could only look at Katy with bewilderment.

"Mary, people talk. Friends talk. It's hard to keep secrets like that."

Emily walked up. "What's wrong?"

"How many people have you told about my issues?"

"I've only talked to you and Judy. But honey, everyone knows. These types of things are hard to keep quiet."

Mary's eyes watered. She took a tissue from her pocket and dabbed her eyes. Linda then walked up.

"What's going on here? Are you okay, Mary?"

Mary couldn't hold the tears in any longer. "Everyone seems to know my secret. I'm scared, embarrassed, and don't know what to do."

"Come sit down on the couch," said Linda as she walked Mary over.

Mary sat down while Katy handed her another tissue.

"This is your fault!" said Katy as she pointed to Emily.

"Kiss my ass," said Emily. "How is this my fault? Have you ever seen me abuse Mary?"

"That's not what I meant."

"So then, how the hell is it my fault? I'm the only one trying to help the poor woman."

"Ladies!" shouted Linda as she held up her hand. "Arguing will not help Mary. Let's all take a breath and sit down. We can talk this out."

The room became quiet as everyone found a place to sit in the living room. Linda sat next to Mary.

"What's going on, Mary?" asked Linda.

Mary used the tissue to wipe her nose. "Yes, I'm in an abusive relationship that I can't get out of. I've tried everything. I don't know why Eric won't divorce me. He certainly doesn't love me. I don't even think he likes me anymore."

"Well, that makes no sense," interrupted Sharon. "You don't need a man's permission to get a divorce. Just file the damn divorce and kick him out of the house!"

"She can't," said Emily. "You don't understand the situation. Eric has a hold on all the finances, the house, everything. Only three people in this room understand what Mary is struggling with. Me, Judy, and Mary."

Others in the room looked toward Judy.

"Oh, come on," continued Emily. "You all talk behind Judy's back about her cheating husband. Except for Katy. Katy brings it up all the time."

Katy frowned. "I do not."

"Yes, you do. Look around the room."

Katy looked at the others. They all nodded their heads yes. Katy sat back in her chair.

"I'm the only one who has tried to help Mary and Judy," continued Emily. "There are ways to get out of bad, abusive marriages without getting the short end of the deal."

"If Mary is being physically abused, all she has to do is call the police," said Sharon. "Domestic abuse might have been tolerated forty years ago. It's not anymore. The police will arrest and charge her husband with assault."

"That sometimes works," said Emily. "But Mary has tried that. Tell them what happened, Mary."

"I can't. If Eric ever found out, he would kill me."

Several gasps could be heard in the room.

"You are safe here, Mary. Am I right?" asked Emily as she looked around the room.

"Yes," said Linda. "Whatever you tell us stays here."

Others nodded yes.

Mary looked frozen, staring at the tile floor.

Emily spoke up. "Mary called the police one time after Eric had beaten her. He was arrested and charged. He behaved during his probation period. However, once his probation was over, Eric took Mary to a construction site and held her over the edge of a deep hole. He forced her to look down and told her, if you ever call the police again, I will bury you under concrete so that no one can find you."

There were more gasps in the room.

"Is that true, Mary?" asked Katy.

Mary looked up. "Yes."

"Has he attacked you since that time?" asked Sharon.

"Mostly, he abuses me verbally and emotionally. However, if he's been drinking and gets angry, he will still hit me. I never know when he will blow up."

"I'm sorry. I've never noticed any injuries, or I would have said something," continued Sharon.

"He knows better than to hit me in the face or head. He usually punches me in my stomach or lower back. The punches to my back hurt the most, and they leave large bruises."

"That's horrible," said Linda. "We have to do something."

"No, it would only make things worse," said Mary.

"We all have to support Mary," said Emily.

"Times have changed. You should report this to the police," suggested Linda.

"No," said Mary. "That would only make it worse."

"I agree with Mary," said Emily. "She's tried the traditional routes. Now we need to be creative."

"What about Judy?" asked Katy. "She suffers emotional abuse from Jack's ongoing affairs."

"Why can't Judy get a divorce?" asked Sharon.

"I could," said Judy. "I've looked into it, but I'm afraid I wouldn't be able to live the lifestyle I'm used to. I also don't want my children to lose most of their inheritance. He would fight for our larger home in Washington, where his primary practice is. He could also defer his salary to limit the amount I would get in alimony."

"Have you tried counseling?" asked Sharon.

"I have a monthly meeting with a therapist. I've asked Jack to join me in therapy, but he wants nothing to do with that. His argument is that he works hard and provides for me. He thinks that should keep me happy. But the reality is that I feel lonely."

"Do you better understand what these two women are enduring?" asked Emily.

The group collectively agreed by either saying yes or nodding their heads.

"What are you hiding, Emily?" asked Katy.

"I'm not hiding anything. Why would you ask that?" said Emily.

"I find it suspicious that six weeks after your husband dies, you move in with another man. Were you having an affair?"

"That's insulting. Bill and I were friends. After Fred died, Bill helped me work through my grief. In doing so, we grew close and started dating. Bill suggested I sell my house and move in with him."

"Jerry heard rumors about you and Bill before Fred's death."

"I think that's enough," said Linda. "We don't need to be turning on each other. This is supposed to be a friendly, social group."

Emily held up her hand and glared at Katy. "What did your husband tell you?"

"Apparently, Fred had shared with some pickleball friends that he suspected you were hooking up with a fire department captain. Bill Hutchins is the fire department captain, isn't he?"

"Fred had no idea what I was doing. He was engaged in his pickleball, softball, poker club, and drinking with friends. He had no time for me. I didn't suffer physical abuse like Mary or feelings of inadequacy like Judy, but I suffered loneliness."

"That doesn't answer the question," stated Katy.

"I met Bill in our first year when I worked as a part-time nurse at Banner Medical Center. We were friends only. Now tell us what Jerry has done to make you such a bitch."

Katy stood up in anger and walked toward Emily.

Linda and Mary both jumped in front of Katy. "That's enough," said Linda. "Sit back down."

"Let her come after me," said Emily. "She's five-two and, from the looks of it, hasn't worked out in years. If Katy thinks she can take on a woman of my skills, let her go."

"You can schedule your battle at the gym. There'll be no fighting here," said Linda.

Once everyone had sat back down, Linda addressed the group. "Let's remember, we are all friends here. Two of our members need our support. Let's focus on that."

"Linda's right," said Sharon. "We should be able to have civil conversations. How can we support Mary and Judy?"

The room was silent for ten uncomfortable seconds.

Emily finally spoke. "Marriages don't have to end in divorce."

"No, they can end in death, right?" asked Katy.

"That's right. Death can be both natural and accidental. Or, a couple might get an annulment."

"You were just lucky that Fred had an accident," replied Katy.

"Katy!" said Sharon. "You shouldn't call her lucky because her husband died."

"I'm just being realistic based on what Emily told us. Emily was lonely because of a lack of attention from her husband. Instead of going through a divorce and losing half of her estate, Fred has an accident, and she keeps everything. And now she has a new boyfriend. I'd call that lucky."

Emily scanned the room to gauge the reaction of others.

"I suppose that's one way to look at it," said Judy.

"It's not the first time, either," said Katy.

"What do you mean?" asked Judy.

"Fred shared with the guys that Emily had been married twice before."

"Is that true?" asked Linda.

"It is," replied Emily.

"How did your other marriages end?"

"Scott Ridley was my first husband. We got married when I was twenty. After four years, we both agreed it wasn't working and got divorced. Ten years later, I married Chuck Landowski. We were married for eight years before he died of liver failure. I then married Fred when I was forty-four. We were married for twenty-two years before his tragic accident."

"I assume you received all the money and property from each marriage?" asked Judy.

"In the first marriage, there was nothing to split. We didn't even own a home. In my last two marriages, I was the sole beneficiary."

"You must be doing okay," said Judy.

"Yes, Judy, I am. That's what I'd like to see for you and Mary."

"Jack is very healthy. I don't expect he will die anytime soon."

"If you're serious about getting out of your marriage, there are ways to speed that process along."

"What are you saying, Emily?" asked Sharon.

"Men sometimes get sick and die, especially older men. There are ways to arrange that."

"Arrange what?"

"Help them along in the process of dying."

"I don't like where this conversation is headed," said Sharon. "I'm going home to read a book."

"Goodnight, Sharon," said Linda as Sharon left through the front door. Linda then turned to Emily. "What ARE you talking about, Emily?"

"Hear me out," said Emily. "Some men are jackasses. Yet, as women, we try to make our marriages work. When the marriages fail, women are often burdened with raising kids on a meager income. Or, in the case of being older, having their quality of life drastically degraded. It's not fair. Why should men benefit from treating women poorly?"

"They shouldn't," agreed Judy.

"No, they shouldn't," said Emily. "As women, sometimes the legal process works against us. In cases of abuse or neglect, sometimes taking matters into our own hands is the smart way to go."

"Was Fred's fall really an accident?" asked Katy.

Everyone in the room looked at Emily in anticipation of her response.

"If you're asking whether I killed Fred, the answer is no."

"What about your second husband?" asked Katy.

"I already told you he died of a liver condition."

"Then what is this talk about helping the process? You're talking nonsense."

"Creating a situation in which an accident may occur differs from murdering someone. I can help Judy and Mary escape their marriages if they so desire."

"By setting up an accident?"

"Or an illness."

"Isn't that the definition of murder?" asked Linda.

"It's the definition of survival," said Emily. "Murder is much too harsh for what we are talking about."

Judy looked at Mary. "You're awfully quiet, Mary. What do you think?"

"I want to be free from Eric. Thirty-six years of his abuse is enough. Even our four children want me to leave him."

"Then you need to leave him," said Linda.

"Emily has already told you why I can't just leave him. I would be penniless. And I don't think he would handle me filing for a divorce any better than if I called the police. His threat was real."

"What about you, Judy?" asked Katy. "Are you ready to be free of Jack?"

"I am. With all of Jack's cheating, I no longer love the man."

"Anyone else here wants to eliminate her husband?" Katy barked while scanning the room.

"Stop it, Katy," said Linda. "No one else wants to be rid of her husband."

"Maritza's not here. Maybe she does."

"Maritza and Ricardo are happily married. You know that."

"I'm just trying to get an accurate count of how many men we need to kill."

"Stop it, Katy. This isn't the Cactus View Murderer's Club."

Katy turned to Emily. "Isn't that what we're talking about? Killing husbands?"

"As I explained earlier, an accident or illness is not the same as murder."

"You're talking in riddles. My guess is you've killed two of your husbands for the money."

"I can assure you the cause of death on Chuck Landowski's death certificate will show liver disease. And Fred's cause of death was reported in the papers as an accident."

"Doesn't mean it's true," replied Katy.

"Maybe not," agreed Emily. "But does it matter? I am financially secure and free of awful marriages. That's the bottom line."

"Ray researched the news articles," said Linda. "He said the investigation hasn't been closed on Fred's death."

"Nothing unusual about that," said Emily. "The police are only being thorough. They've already interviewed me twice now. I have nothing to fear."

"I understand what Emily is saying," offered Judy. "She creates a way to get out of a marriage without being held responsible for whatever happens."

"I'm to the point of not caring what happens. I just want out," said Mary.

"We've all read stories of women poisoning their husbands over time," said Katy.

Just then, the doorbell rang. Linda walked to the door and opened it. "Maritza, you made it."

"Yes. I asked Ricardo to drop me off after the show so I could see everyone. I'm glad you're all still here."

"How was the show?"

"It was terrific. If anyone wants to see it, tickets are still available for the Thursday and Friday shows. What have I missed?"

"We've just been talking about killing our husbands," said Katy in a loud voice.

"What!?"

"We've all been reading too many crime thrillers," said Linda. "I think our next book should be a love story. Come on in and sit down. We're discussing how to help Mary and Judy escape their marriages while still having the means to live well."

"I see," said Maritza. "Maybe I should have skipped the show."

"No, you made the right choice," said Linda.

"Catch me up," said Maritza.

"You know the situation with Mary and Judy. They are both in terrible marriages. We've been discussing ways to end the marriages without them ending up in the poorhouse. Both husbands are very controlling, although in separate ways. Mary's is emotionally and physically abusive, while Judy's husband can't keep his hands and other parts off other women."

"Ricardo is not a divorce attorney, but he knows some good ones," offered Maritza.

"We don't need attorneys for what Emily is talking about," said Katy.

"You really should be represented by someone," insisted Maritza while looking at Judy and Mary.

"They want their husbands to die from a disease or an accident," said Katy.

"I don't understand," said Maritza.

"We're just having a discussion on ways to be free from abusive husbands without going through a messy divorce," explained Emily.

"Emily seems to be an expert," laughed Katy.

"I've been through it, that's all," responded Emily. "We are simply trying to help Judy and Mary."

"Emily wants to create a situation where their husbands either die from sickness or an unfortunate accident," said Katy.

"That would be easier, wouldn't it?" asked Maritza.

Linda was shocked to hear Maritza say such a thing. "You would be okay with that?"

"Not really. It's not something I would do, but I've certainly seen what Mary has endured. After talking to my husband about her situation, I realized her choices were not the best. Either live as a penniless spinster or live without fear and with lots of money. If you can kill the bastard and be free, what the hell? Can you tell I don't like the man?" laughed Maritza.

"What about Jack?" asked Linda.

"I don't see it as the same situation," said Maritza. "Being cheated on is difficult, but not the same as being physically and psychologically abused. A jury might not be so sympathetic."

"If it's an accident or illness, a jury will never hear about it," said Emily.

"It's a dangerous game, Emily. With today's forensic science and technological advances, it's hard to get away with anything," warned Maritza.

"Emily's done it twice," interrupted Katy.

Maritza looked at Emily. "Is that true?"

"I haven't gotten away with anything. My second husband had a liver condition, and you already know about Fred's accident."

"Give us an example of what you are talking about," said Judy. "Tell us one way you would make a man sick without the doctors or police finding out."

"I'm sure you've all learned about ways in the books we've read. And that's what we're talking about. The books we've read, right?"

Some in the room nodded yes. Emily continued. "It has to be done in a manner that does not raise suspicion. For example, a long-term illness would not raise the same suspicion as a quick death might. You would not want to use a quick-acting poison. Let's say you used anti-freeze as your choice of poison.

The key would be to do it over time. Your husband would be ill for several months. Only if the police suspected a poisoning would they test for it."

"Is that what you used with your second husband?" asked Katy.

"No."

"What did you use?"

"Katy, if you ever do such a thing, the next critical part is never admitting to or sharing what you did with anyone."

Emily could see members looking around the room at each other, trying to gauge their reactions.

"Alright," announced Linda. "It's getting late, and I think we've heard enough talk of murder and such. Next time we meet, let's vow to only talk about the book we've read. I won't sleep tonight after this awkward discussion."

"I think our genre of books is warping our minds," said Maritza.

"Maybe so," agreed Judy.

Linda ushered everyone out the door. "Be careful driving home, ladies."

Chapter 9

The following morning, Detectives Lou Begay and Leland Ashford met Surprise Detective Dan Baxter at their favorite breakfast joint, Richi's Diner. After ordering breakfast, they discussed the Fred Levine case.

"Where are you at on the case?" asked Baxter.

"I'm kind of stuck. I've got enough to suspect Emily Settlemire of murder, but I can't prove it," said Begay.

"What did her new boyfriend tell you?"

"Nothing. Hutchins wouldn't agree to an interview."

"I wonder what he's afraid of?" said Baxter.

"He wasn't happy about my interview with Emily."

"Wasn't he a friend of Fred's?

"Yes. Bill was a friend to both Fred and Emily."

"If he's not talking, my guess is they were sleeping together before the accident," said Baxter.

"That wouldn't surprise me at all. I need to find someone who knows and will tell me," said Begay.

Ashford spoke up. "I checked with the first responding officers, as you requested. No one saw anyone else on the trail when they arrived."

Baxter shook his head. "I would have guessed Emily wasn't the only other person on that hike."

"We're not giving up on that theory yet," said Begay.

"Have we done any DNA testing?" asked Ashford.

"What are you thinking?" said Begay.

"You said Levine was likely pushed off that mountain. What type of clothing was he wearing?"

"He had on what I would call hiking shorts and a t-shirt. A light windbreaker was tied around his waist."

"The t-shirt was probably made of cotton," continued Ashford. "What was the temperature that day?"

"I remember it was still warm when I arrived. I didn't need a jacket."

"Wait a second," said Baxter as he messed with his phone. "Let's see, the last Monday in September. Here it is. The high temperature on that day was eighty-six degrees and sunny."

"Okay," said Ashford. "It's likely anyone hiking that trail would be sweating. If someone pushed Levine, it's possible that person left some DNA on that shirt."

"If the DNA belongs to Emily, it might not be any help. She could easily explain that," said Begay.

"No, but what if it belongs to Bill Hutchins?" asked Ashford.

"It would be harder to explain," answered Begay.

"Have you tested it?" asked Baxter.

"There was no need to until you analyzed the disturbance on that mountain," said Begay. "I'll send the clothing to the Central Regional Crime lab for analysis first thing Monday."

"Anymore background on Hutchins?" asked Baxter.

"You know he's a retired fire captain. From all accounts, he was an exemplary employee. He's been divorced from his only wife for eight years. Apparently, he met Emily through Fred. Fred and Bill were pickleball buddies."

"I was hoping for some salacious, dirty information on Bill. It would make him a better suspect."

"I haven't found any yet."

"You need to talk to Emily's girlfriends," suggested Baxter.

"It's on my list," said Begay.

After breakfast and their second cup of coffee, Baxter wished Begay and Ashford good luck as they left the restaurant.

Mary and Judy continued discussing the book club meeting throughout the day on Thursday. Every time one of them had another comment or question, they would call the other. They were both intrigued and frightened by the conversations.

"Emily wants to meet tomorrow for coffee," said Mary. "She scares me."

"She scares me too," said Judy. "But there is a burning desire in my gut to hear more. I don't want to kill anyone, but I want to hear her ideas."

"Yes, I feel the same way. It's hard to explain, but the thought of being free from Eric gives me hope."

"My situation is not as bad as yours, Mary, but I don't want to live like this anymore. I'm thinking of filing for divorce and just accepting the financial consequences."

"You at least need to listen to what she has to say. Jack is the one who should pay, not you."

"Yes, I'm okay with hearing her out."

"Good, I'll let her know we will meet at ten o'clock at the Casa Café."

"See you then."

At 10:00 a.m. the following morning, Emily was already seated at a corner table with three cups of coffee when Mary and Judy walked in. Emily was dressed more casually this day. She was wearing a black top and black capris.

"You bought us coffee?" asked Mary.

"Yes. With cream and one sugar for you and black for Judy. Did I get it right?"

"You did!" said Mary.

"I'm happy you agreed to meet again. I wasn't sure after Wednesday's book club meeting. That was wild."

"It got a little tense," agreed Judy.

"That's why I wanted to talk away from the group. We don't have to be so discreet."

"We want to know exactly what you have in mind with this accident and illness talk," said Judy.

"How far will you go to get out of an awful marriage?" asked Emily.

"I'm not sure," said Judy. "But I'm here to listen."

"Me too," agreed Mary.

"Okay, let's start with Mary. How much would it mean to be free from Eric?"

"I've been with him so long, it's hard to imagine. To be free from fear would be life-changing."

"How about you, Judy?" asked Emily.

"Well, I'm not in any danger of physical abuse like Mary is. But the heartache and emotional abuse of Jack's ongoing affairs can be overwhelming. There are times when I cry myself to sleep."

"I empathize with both of you. I've gone through the same emotions. It wasn't until I took control of my situation that I became happy again."

"Emily, on Wednesday, you talked about murder," said Judy.

"I didn't use that term. We are only talking about natural deaths and accidents. Never think of a natural death or accident as murder."

"Alright, tell me how Jack dies a natural death?"

"There are many ways. However, it must be in a manner that no one, especially the police, believes it is anything but a natural death."

"Okay, give us an example."

"One of the most commonly used methods is making someone sick through the use of anti-freeze fluid."

"Anti-freeze?" asked Mary.

"Yes. Many people keep some stored in their garage. You can buy it almost anywhere. When consumed, it will make you sick. Take enough of it, and you will die."

"Wouldn't that be easily discovered during an autopsy?" asked Judy.

"It's possible if that is something the medical examiner is looking for."

"Wouldn't that always be something they look for?"

"Not necessarily. If done properly, there won't even be an autopsy."

"You said if done properly. What does that entail?"

"If the deceased has been ill over time and has been under a doctor's care, an autopsy is not always done."

"But how do you pull that off?" asked Judy.

"Slowly."

"And how do you do that?"

"Okay, we are talking hypothetically, correct?"

Both women nodded yes.

"Let's say you wanted Jack to die naturally. After selecting the proper medication, you would give it to him in small amounts. It might be in a drink or mixed with some food. Just enough to make him feel ill. Maybe nauseous. Not enough to send him to a doctor or hospital. You continue this for a few weeks, slowly increasing the dosage. If he doesn't go himself, you encourage him to see a doctor. The doctor is going to assume Jack has some intestinal bug or something. He might do some blood tests. A doctor is not testing for anti-freeze. And if you time it right, there will be none in his system when he goes to the doctor."

Both Mary and Judy were intently listening to Emily talk.

Emily continued. "You keep this routine up, gradually increasing the dose. Jack will become increasingly sick. The doctor will take a guess at what is ailing Jack and probably prescribe something. Maybe you even take him to the emergency room after a heavier dose. He will be in severe pain. Once his record of illness is established, it's easier to give the final dose without raising suspicion. Everyone will know he had been under a doctor's care before his death. The police will hardly give it a second look."

"If the doctors didn't know what killed him, wouldn't they test for poisons?" asked Mary.

"It depends. That's why the path to death has to be believable. Remember during COVID when it seemed anyone who died was ruled a COVID death?"

"Yeah, I remember that," said Judy.

"I was still working as a nurse during COVID. If it wasn't a traffic accident or something, hospitals ruled everything a COVID death. They were then compensated by the government."

"Huh?" said Mary.

"Yeah, hospitals were getting paid for every COVID death. Don't you think they wanted to get as much money as possible from the government? For all I know, they may still get paid. If you look at the data during the pandemic, all other causes of death dropped significantly. It was the best time to create a natural death."

The conversation was making Judy nervous. She tried not to let anyone see her shivering. "I'm going to get another coffee. Would either of you like another one?" asked Judy.

Both women said yes. Judy got up and walked to the counter for refills.

"Judy seems nervous," stated Emily.

"I'm nervous as well. I've never had a conversation like this before," replied Mary.

"No, but I'll bet you've thought of ways to be free from Eric."

Mary looked down. "I have. I can't say I've thought of murder, but I've thought of what my life might be without him in it."

"Mary, don't use the term murder. Natural death or accident is how we must view these things."

"Right, I'm sorry."

"It's a mindset, Mary."

Judy returned to the table with refills for everyone.

"Are you okay, Judy?" asked Emily.

"Yeah, I'm fine. This stuff is hard to talk about."

"It's harder to live a life of unhappiness."

"I suppose. Did you use anti-freeze to fuel your second husband's natural death?"

"I like how you are using the correct terminology, Judy. But, no. I did not use anti-freeze. Remember, he died from liver failure. I used a better method."

"So, you're giving us advice that you've never used yourself?"

"All I said is I didn't use anti-freeze. Unless someone is looking for it, I used something better and less detectable."

"Are you going to share what it was?"

"Amanita Phalloides."

"Huh?"

"It's a mushroom. Also known as the death cap."

"You poisoned him with mushrooms?" asked Mary.

"I used mushrooms to help create the symptoms that led to his death. It is one of the most poisonous mushrooms in the world. And the best part is they look similar to edible mushrooms. Makes for a good cover story."

"Where do you get them?" asked Judy.

"Fry's supermarket."

"What!?"

Emily laughed. "You find them in the wild. You can even find them in Arizona."

"Your second husband died naturally from eating poisonous mushrooms?" asked Judy.

"Yes. These are so much better than other poisons."

"Why is that?"

"Even if the doctors or coroner do an autopsy and figure it out, all they can say is that the victim ate poisonous mushrooms. That finding would, of course, be supported by the spouse saying he had collected wild mushrooms. It gives you a great cover story."

"I can see how that would work," agreed Mary. "How do you know so much?"

"Oh, I do my research."

"Be quiet!" said Judy.

Katy Cullen walked up to the table. "Well, hello there. How are the three of you doing today?"

"We're just fine, Katy," said Emily. "How are you?"

"Me? I'm great. What's the discussion for today? How to get away with murder?"

"Stop, Katy," said Emily. "We are simply having coffee."

"Uh-huh. You're not so dressed up today, Emily. I see that black must be your favorite color."

"Yeah, and I like the Sun Devils sweatshirt you're wearing. Stylish," responded Emily.

"Thank you, Emily. Well, hope you ladies figure things out. Good seeing you," said Katy as she walked away.

"Sorry," said Judy. "Katy can be obnoxious."

"Don't worry about it. I can handle Katy."

"If one of our husbands dies, Katy could be a problem," said Judy.

"Not if she knows nothing," responded Emily.

"We talked about getting rid of husbands at our club meeting."

"It's a crime thriller book club. Of course, we talk about murder and ways to get away with murder. We discuss that all the time. It doesn't mean we commit murder. If you ever need it, the book club is another brilliant cover."

Judy cocked her head. "I never thought of it like that."

"You also talked about accidents," said Mary.

"Yes, that's another avenue you can take. Accidents are probably easier to explain and cover-up. There are all different ways accidents can occur."

"That's how Fred died, isn't it?"

"Yes, he died from an accident."

"Did you push him off the mountain?"

"What did I talk about earlier, Mary? If I pushed him off, I would be stupid to tell anyone that. You must not tell anyone if you decide to facilitate a death. Never admit to anything other than what you intend it to be. If it's an accident, it's an accident. Do you understand what I'm saying?"

Mary nodded. "I so want to be rid of Eric. But I don't know if I can do what you can, Emily."

"If you can't, there's another way."

"Another way?"

"I know a guy that could help you."

"Help me? How?"

"Tell him what you want, and he will do the dirty work."

"Are you talking about hiring an assassin?" asked Judy.

"I hate that word," replied Emily. "Let's call him a marriage counselor."

Judy couldn't help but laugh. "You want Mary to hire a marriage counselor to kill her husband?"

"I want nothing. Right now, I'm your marriage counselor, providing you with options. Only you can decide what you want."

"How much would it cost to get this help?" asked Mary.

"If you want Eric removed from your life forever, I'd say about twenty thousand dollars."

"Oh, my god. I don't have access to that kind of money. Eric controls all the money."

"Okay, so that option is off the table for you."

"This is all just talk, right?" asked Judy.

"Of course," said Emily.

"Hypothetically, how do you use the mushrooms?" asked Mary.

Emily smiled. "Well, hypothetically, you would grind them up and mix them with his food."

"You would do it a little at a time?"

"It depends. Does Eric like mushrooms?"

"Yes."

"Then let's say you and Eric go on a hike to collect mushrooms. Amanita Phalloides look similar to edible wood mushrooms. Many people accidentally die from the misidentification of this mushroom. One mushroom is enough to kill a human being. The poisons attack the kidneys and liver. No one would ever know it was anything but an accident."

Mary and Judy looked at each other.

"It sounds too easy," pondered Judy.

"It is easy," replied Emily. "No one will ever know, and you will be free from the cheating jackass."

"Where do you find these mushrooms?" asked Judy.

"At higher elevations, especially after monsoon season. I've found them up near Prescott and Cottonwood. I've heard the best place for mushroom hunting is around Pinewood and Show Low, northeast of here."

"If I were to do something, I like the mushroom idea," said Judy. "How would the police know it wasn't accidental?"

"You're catching on, Judy."

"I like that idea as well," agreed Mary.

"Only one of you can use the mushroom plan."

"Why is that?" asked Mary.

"Think about it. You are both friends and belong to the same book club. If your husbands die of the same method, don't you think that would arouse suspicion?"

After a pause, "Oh, I see your point," said Mary.

"If Judy goes through with this, you need a different plan, Mary. Eric is older than Jack. Having an accident would be more believable for Eric."

"Why didn't you use the mushrooms on Fred?" asked Judy. "It sounds easier that way."

"Never use the same method twice."

"Oh, yeah. That makes sense."

"I can't think of how I would create an accident with Eric," pondered Mary.

"What does Eric like to do?" asked Emily.

"He likes to drink."

"What does he like to drink?"

"Anything, but usually beer or bourbon in the evening."

"How much does he drink in the evening?"

"Anywhere from two to five drinks, depending on his mood."

"Do you regularly have sleeping pills in your home?"

"Yeah. I occasionally need them to fall asleep, especially after being abused."

"Then what about suicide?"

"Suicide? I don't think he would do that."

"What if you filed for divorce?"

Mary sighed. "That might get me killed, Emily. Even if I got a divorce, I would have no money to live on."

"I'm not talking about getting a divorce. You file for one without telling Eric. It will take a week or so for the paperwork to go through. You then spike his bourbon with enough sleeping pills to kill him. You can then add some mushroom powder to ensure his death. The cover story is that he was so depressed he took his own life. And with alcohol and barbiturates in his system, no one will even think to look for anything else."

Mary was silent for several seconds. "I suppose it might work. But why the mushroom powder?"

"Today's sleeping pills aren't as potent as in years past. The mushroom is added assurance Eric dies. You don't want him to survive only to deny taking any sleeping pills."

"That's a good point," said Mary. "You seem to think of everything, Emily."

"This is serious business. It's important to think of everything."

"We have a lot to think about," said Mary.

"Yes, you do. Don't decide lightly. But if you want to move forward, I will help you. Now, I've got to get going to my salon appointment. I'll talk to you two later."

"Bye, Emily," said Judy.

After Emily had left, Mary looked at Judy. "What do you think of all that?"

"It's a lot to take in. As unhappy as I am, I'm unsure I can do anything like this. What about you, Mary?"

"Judy, I don't feel like I have another viable choice if I want a future life."

"I understand," said Judy while nodding. "Don't rush into anything, and be careful."

Chapter 10

It was 10:15 a.m. the following Tuesday, and Bill Hutchins was playing drop-in pickleball at the Cactus View pickleball courts. It was easy to pick him out with his red Mesa Fire Department hat. Hutchins finished scoring a point with a sharp backhanded slap down the line. Turning toward the baseline, Hutchins noticed a dark-haired man in a blue wind-breaker watching the game from the breezeway. As he got closer to the back of the court, he recognized the man as Detective Lou Begay. The appearance of Begay distracted Hutchins, causing him to miss his last four shots. After the game, Hutchins walked out into the breezeway.

"What are you doing here, Detective?" asked Hutchins.

"I'm watching you play pickleball."

"Yes, but why?"

"I'm investigating Fred Levine's death. I need to learn as much as possible about the people who knew him. You won't talk to me, so I've got to find out who your friends are. Maybe they can help me out."

"This is harassment, Detective. I want you to stop following me around."

Begay chuckled. "Harassment? I'm just standing here watching a game of pickleball. You're the one who approached me."

"I already talked to you early in the investigation."

"Yes, but now I have more questions. But hey, I understand you don't want to be involved. But I'll be talking to people who know you."

"Okay, I'll answer your questions. We can walk over to the clubhouse."

"No. If you want to talk, meet me at the Sheriff's Department at one o'clock."

"Alright, I'll be there at one o'clock."

Begay turned and walked toward the parking lot. Hutchins was too rattled to play any more pickleball. He packed up his stuff and rode his golf cart home. He stepped in the front door and found Emily talking on the phone. She was surprised to see Bill home early. She quickly ended her call.

"Why are you home so early?" Emily asked.

"That damn detective showed up."

"What detective?"

"Begay!"

"Detective Begay came to the pickleball courts?"

"Yes."

"What did he want?"

"He said since I wouldn't talk to him, he needed to find out who my friends were so he could talk to them."

"So you left?"

"Yeah. It shook me up. Now I need to go to the Sheriff's Department at one o'clock for another interview."

"You said you wouldn't talk anymore."

"That was before Detective Begay started stalking me."

"He's just trying to get under your skin, Bill. It will help if you remain calm. Stick to the story."

"Yeah, I know that. But being a retired fire chief, I have a reputation to uphold. I don't want people believing I'm involved."

"Just be yourself and answer the questions the same as last time. Let me fix you some lunch."

"No thanks. I'm not hungry."

Hutchins arrived early for the interview. He sat in the waiting area for ten minutes before Detective Begay opened the door leading into the detective bureau.

"Thank you for coming, Bill. Follow me," said Begay.

Hutchins followed Begay down a brightly lit hallway. They approached a door that opened into a box-like room with gray-painted walls. A small metal table sat on one side of the room. Hutchins noticed a camera mounted on the opposite wall. A microphone sat on the table.

"Please have a seat over there," said Begay, pointing to a metal chair on the table's far side.

"Thank you for coming, Bill. You are not under arrest, and you are not being detained against your will. Do you understand?"

"Yes."

"And you are voluntarily here to answer some questions. Is that correct?"

"Yes."

"We need to clarify some things about Fred Levine's death. Please tell me again what Emily told you," said Begay.

"It's simple, really. Emily said they were hiking up White Tank Mountain. She was leading the way, and Fred was following her. Emily heard a yell and looked back to see Fred falling down the mountain."

"Did she say how he fell?"

"She didn't see him fall."

"Why did they go so late in the day?"

"You'll have to ask Emily."

"You haven't talked about Fred's death with her?"

"Yes, but not about things like that."

"Has Emily mentioned anyone else going on the hike with them?"

"No."

"What if I told you there is evidence of a third person being there?"

"I, uh, I have not heard that."

"Who do you think that might have been?"

"I have no idea. I never heard about a third person."

"Where did you first meet Emily?"

"It was a party at Fred's house."

"And how did you know Fred?"

"We met playing pickleball."

"When did you date Emily?"

"I wasn't dating Emily."

"You're living with her, correct?"

"Well, yeah, now we are. But not before the accident."

"I didn't ask about before the accident. Why did you assume that?"

"Oh, I don't know. I didn't assume. I just misunderstood."

"Uh-huh. How soon after the accident did you and Emily start dating?"

"Six weeks."

"Six weeks?"

"Yes, I've told you this before."

"Well, I know you moved in together six weeks after Fred's death. I assumed you must have dated a few times before deciding to move in together."

"Uh, yeah, we probably did."

"You don't remember?"

"No, I mean yeah. We dated a few times."

"Bill, I've talked to some people who know you and Emily. They believe you and Emily were having an affair prior to Fred's death."

"No, we were just friends. Fred was my friend as well."

"Just friends with benefits?"

"NO! We did not start seeing each other until after Fred's accident. Maybe some thought we were because we were friends. I don't know."

"Bill, you can see how this looks suspicious. You date Fred's wife soon after his death and then move in together at your house."

"Emily was hurting. I was the one who helped her get over her emotional distress."

"You've admitted to dating Emily a few times before she moved in with you. Even if that was only two weeks before, that means she started dating you only four weeks after Fred's death. And I'm being generous on the timeline here, Bill."

Begay noticed Bill was nervous. He observed his Adam's apple move as he swallowed. Bill was also rapidly tapping the heel of his right foot on the floor.

"We weren't having an affair."

"Bill, you're a retired fire captain. You've been around crime scenes, right?"

"Yes, lots of times."

"You have some information on how the police investigate crime scenes, right?"

"Yes."

"You know we don't take what we see as the truth. We work at a crime scene to find the story left by the evidence. Correct?"

"Yeah."

"Well, I'm going to share with you something we know. Based on analysis of the scene, someone pushed Fred off the mountain."

"What?"

"He fell ten feet away from the side of the hill and did not hit the ground until about twenty feet down the hill. That doesn't happen from tripping and falling over the edge."

Bill was silent. Begay let the silence hang in the air before continuing.

"Did you push Fred off that mountain, Bill?"

"No!"

"Then who did?"

Begay could see Bill lick his lips and swallow hard. His right foot was still moving, and he was now staring at the table.

"Who pushed him, Bill?"

After several more seconds. "All I know is what Emily told me."

"Now is the time to tell the truth, Bill. We are conducting DNA tests on Fred's clothing. Will your DNA be on that shirt?"

"I don't know how it could be. Unless I had touched that shirt sometime when he wore it before the accident."

"Was anyone else with Emily that day?"

"No."

"If you weren't there, how do you know that?"

"What?"

"How would you know nobody else was there?"

"I don't know. That's what Emily told me."

"Did Emily share with you what would happen that day?"

"No. How could she? She didn't know he would fall."

"He was pushed, remember?"

"Yeah, I don't know that. That's what you say."

"That's what the evidence says, Bill."

"I don't have any other information. Are we about done?"

"Why are you so nervous?"

"Because you are accusing me of killing Fred."

"I've noticed Emily likes to talk. I'll bet she has shared what really happened with someone else. What do you think, Bill?"

"She's told lots of people about Fred's accident."

"I'm talking about what really happened that day. Women like to talk things out. You know that. The truth will be found."

"Can I go now?" asked Bill.

"Sure. Let me walk you out."

Hutchins didn't say another word as Begay walked him out. "Thank you for coming in," said Begay as he watched Hutchins walk away.

Twenty minutes later, Hutchins arrived home. He walked in to find Emily talking on her phone. Emily immediately recognized Bill was in distress. She ended her phone call.

"Bill, what's wrong?"

"Detective Begay believes I had something to do with Fred's death."

"How can that be?"

"He says there is evidence of Fred being pushed off the trail."

"What type of evidence?"

"He didn't say."

"That's because he's bluffing," replied Emily.

"It didn't sound like he was bluffing!"

"What possible evidence could he have to indicate Fred was pushed?"

"How the hell would I know!?" shouted Bill. "You said this would be easy to sell. It's not sounding so easy now!"

"Bill, calm down. It's going to be okay. The police always do this type of thing. Detective Begay is grabbing at straw theories, hoping one of them will be right. Did he say there was a witness?"

"No."

"See, he's bluffing."

"They're testing Fred's clothing for DNA. What if they find my DNA on his clothing?"

"They won't find any DNA. And even if they do, Fred was a friend you played pickleball with. Your cover is that you played with him that morning before our hike. You probably touched him during play. If they ask me, I will tell them Fred didn't change his shirt because he knew he would get sweaty again on the hike."

"We didn't play pickleball that morning."

"It doesn't matter. Would anyone remember if Fred played on a Monday in September?"

"No, I suppose not."

"See? It's going to be okay."

"Emily, the detective said Fred first hit the mountainside twenty feet down."

"So what? That proves nothing."

"Maybe not, but he's investigating me now. You assured me this would go without a hitch. I'd call this a big hitch!" screamed Bill.

"Did he arrest you?"

"No."

"Then he has nothing. If they had evidence you were involved, you'd be in jail. This is typical police work."

"I knew you shouldn't have moved in so soon."

"Do you want me to move out?"

"It's too late now."

Emily huffed and walked out of the room.

Chapter 11

Emily met Chris Molina on Friday for lunch at the Village Inn, off Grand Avenue. Emily first met Chris when she was volunteering at one of the local emergency medical clinics. Chris was a twenty-three-year-old white male. He was thin with a shaved head. His attire for the day was an AC/DC t-shirt and jeans. Chris had been a patient at the clinic for a drug overdose and various other ailments. Emily invited Chris to lunch on her dime.

"How have you been doing, Chris?"

"I've been sober for five months now."

"That's excellent. I'm happy for you."

After some more small talk, Chris asked, "Why did you ask me to lunch?"

"I might have a job for you," replied Emily. "But only if you still do the type of work I need."

"What do you need?"

"Nothing right now, but I may need you to take someone out. Is that something you still do?"

"By out, you mean to kill them?"

Emily nodded yes.

"I've only killed once before," said Chris.

"Are you interested?" asked Emily.

"Depends. Who is it, and how much would you be willing to pay?"

"Who it is doesn't matter right now. But if I needed to, I could pay you twenty thousand dollars in cash."

"That's not enough," responded Chris.

"How much would it take?"

"Are we talking about someone well-known or important?"

"No. Just an everyday person who might be a problem for me."

Chris thought for a moment. "I could do it for fifty thousand in cash."

"Fifty thousand? That's a lot of money, Chris."

"The risk of killing someone is extreme. Fifty thousand is a bargain."

Emily looked down at the table. She had hardly touched her food. "Okay, if I need you, I'll pay you fifty thousand."

"Deal," said Chris as he devoured his last bite. "Call me on my phone if you decide to move forward." He then got up and walked out.

Emily sat staring at her food, thinking about her next move. I better get the money out now, thought Emily. If I need to take action, I don't want the police to find a significant withdrawal just days before the murder.

Emily finished her water and left without eating. She paid the cashier on the way out.

The next day, Linda, Maritza, Sharon, and Katy met for afternoon ice cream at the Casa Café. The afternoon was warm, so they sat outside under an umbrella table.

"Is anyone else coming?" asked Sharon.

"I only invited the three of you," answered Linda. "The last book club meeting went in a direction I hadn't expected. The four of us didn't have time to visit much. I thought we could chat before next week's meeting."

"Well, you picked a great sunny afternoon," replied Sharon.

Maritza and Katy agreed. The four women chatted about their past week's activities, various ailments, and the stupid things their husbands did.

As they finished their soft-serve ice cream, Katy changed the subject.

"I saw Mary, Judy, and Emily having coffee together a few days ago," said Katy.

"They provide each other support," said Linda.

"I think they were plotting against their husbands."

"Just because they talked about their husbands at the meeting doesn't mean that's all they talk about," said Maritza.

"True, but it was their demeanor when I asked them about it. It was like they were talking about something sinister, and they didn't want me to intrude."

"Don't be so cynical, Katy," said Maritza.

"I'm not. But after the conversation during book club, it was interesting to find the three of them together."

"I didn't like where that conversation was going," said Sharon. "In my day, you made the best of your choices. You didn't plot accidents or illnesses against your spouse."

"Were you ever abused?" asked Maritza.

"No," replied Sharon. "I had a good husband."

"Well, not everyone does."

"You don't kill them for it."

"Why did you bring this back up, Katy?" asked Linda.

"I just wanted you to know they were together. I found it quite a coincidence it was just days after our meeting."

"I think Emily is aloof," said Sharon. "She probably doesn't have many good friends."

"You don't know her well enough to judge," said Linda.

"Maybe not. But I didn't get a good vibe about her."

"I think she killed her husband," said Katy.

"He died in a hiking accident," Linda reminded her.

"It was the way she talked about creating accidents or illnesses. She's dangerous," said Katy.

"I don't care for her," said Sharon.

"Give her a chance," said Linda. "Judy liked her enough to invite her to the club. If she doesn't fit in after a couple of months, I will ask her not to come again."

"That's fair," agreed Maritza.

"I'll give her a chance," said Sharon.

"What about you, Katy?" asked Linda.

"Oh, I want to see where this goes. We could have a murder mystery in our own club to solve. It might be fun."

"Let's hope not," said Linda.

"Emily was wearing black again," said Katy.

"So what?" asked Linda.

"She seems to wear black a lot. If I am right about her, she is like a black widow spider. Black and deadly."

"Alright, that's enough," said Linda. "Let's change the subject."

"Thank you," said Sharon.

Meanwhile, Mary was at home serving dinner to Eric. She had fixed one of his favorites, a homemade chicken pot pie. The aroma of freshly baked crust filled the kitchen.

"It's ready," said Mary.

Eric came into the dining room and sat in his usual chair. Mary brought Eric a plate of steaming pot pie and an ice-cold Corona Light. "Looks good," said Eric.

Mary then fixed herself a plate and sat across from Eric, who was already eating. About halfway through the meal, Mary spoke.

"Eric, I need to ask a favor."

Eric looked up. "What kind of favor?"

"I got a call from my mother this morning. She has taken a turn for the worse. I would like to return to Minnesota for only a few weeks to help her move into assisted living."

"A few weeks?"

"Yes. It will take some time to make the arrangements to move her."

"Who would take care of things here?"

"I was hoping you would help and let me go. It's for my mother."

"No, we'll go back together when it's hot here next summer. Then we can see the kids and your mother simultaneously."

"But she needs help now, Eric."

"She'll be fine. I need you here. I told you, next summer."

"But Eric..."

"Damn it, Mary! Don't you listen to me? We've discussed this. That's enough. Now get me another beer."

Mary began to cry. She wiped the tears with her napkin.

"Now what's wrong?" asked Eric in a sarcastic tone.

"Did you ever love me, Eric?"

"What kind of question is that? I married you, didn't I?"

"That's not an answer."

"I worked hard my whole life to provide for you and the kids. The least you could do is to be a good wife now that I'm retired," screamed Eric.

Mary knew not to push too hard for fear that Eric would become violent again. She stood up, walked to the refrigerator, and grabbed another beer for Eric. Mary briskly marched back and placed the beer hard on the table.

"You can open it yourself." Mary then retreated to the bedroom and shut the door. After taking a few deep breaths to calm her crying, Mary picked up her cell phone and called Emily Settlemire.

"Hi, Mary. What's up?"

In a soft voice, Mary said, "I'm ready."

"Ready for what?"

"I'm ready for Eric to die. How do I get some of those mushrooms you were talking about?"

Chapter 12

Mary met with Emily at the local IHOP restaurant the following Monday morning for a late breakfast. The late breakfast was necessitated by Mary having to wait to leave home until Eric had eaten his breakfast and went to play cards with some friends.

"How have things been since Saturday?" asked Emily.

"Very tense," replied Mary. "Eric has been angry with me since I asked to go to Minnesota. I have to be on my best behavior."

"Sorry, Mary. But are you sure you want to do this?"

"Yes. I've been thinking about it since our last conversation. After this week, I'm sure. I can't live like this anymore. Whatever the risk."

Their conversation was interrupted by the waiter who took their order. Emily ordered an omelet with bacon, while Mary ordered buttered toast with her coffee.

"Is that all you're going to have?" asked Emily.

"I haven't had much of an appetite this week."

"I understand. How can I help you?"

"Tell me again where I find these mushrooms you talked about."

Emily reached into her purse, pulled out a small red coin pouch, and handed it to Mary. "There is enough powdered mushroom in this pouch to kill Eric six times over."

Mary grabbed the coin pouch and stuffed it into her larger purse. "Only once will be enough. Tell me again how to use it."

"Are you going to use the suicide scenario?" asked Emily.

"Yes. I think that would work. I don't like the idea of dragging it out over several weeks or months."

"You said you already have prescription sleeping pills?"

"Yes."

"Excellent. What is your plan?"

"I was hoping you could help with that."

Emily nodded. "You said Eric drinks beer and bourbon, correct?"

"Most nights, especially recently. Mostly beer, but sometimes bourbon."

"Then pick a night when he's drinking bourbon. You want him intoxicated as much as possible."

"Alright."

"Before that, you need to crush the pills into fine powder. Use all of them."

"I believe Eric's are gel caps," said Mary.

"Then you open the caps and collect the powder."

Mary nodded, "Okay."

"You'll then be ready to spike his drink."

"How much do I put in?" asked Mary.

"Start with the sleeping pill powder. Put a small amount in his drink to make him drowsy. Once he is already drowsy, it will be harder for him to detect the taste of the mushrooms. After you lure him to the bedroom, you can fix a drink with the remaining sleeping powder and a teaspoon of the mushroom powder. Too much, and Eric might taste the mushroom."

"Okay."

"As I said, wait for a time when he's drinking bourbon. That's stronger and makes the suicide look more intentional. You want his blood alcohol to be as high as possible. Do what you can to encourage him to drink more than usual."

"How would I do that?"

"After he's had a few, offer to have another drink with him. Agree to have sex with him if he'll have another drink with you. That's when you spike the drink. And make your drink very weak and his very strong. A strong drink will cover the taste of the mushroom."

Mary smiles. "I like that."

"Now," said Emily. She then paused as the waiter arrived with their breakfast.

"Can I get you anything else?" the waiter asked.

"We are fine, thank you," replied Emily.

After the waiter left, Emily continued. "This is a crucial part, so listen carefully. Do you have a computer and printer?"

"Eric has both in his office."

"Perfect. Once Eric has passed out, you will need to create a suicide note on his computer. Print the note and set it on the bed or a table beside it."

"What should the note say?"

"Short and simple. Do not type a long note. Have Eric apologize for what he's put you through. After that, you must leave and spend time with someone to provide an alibi."

"I don't know where I'd go."

"Call a friend from the book club and ask to visit. Tell her Eric is drinking and being belligerent. Explain that you need to get clear from Eric for a few hours. That will give you a great alibi witness."

"Can I call you?"

"No. I might not be the best alibi right now. I wouldn't use Judy, either. Maritza would be perfect. If not her, maybe Linda. You need to be upset and let whoever you talk to know you don't want to go home until Eric sobers up. When you eventually leave, go to a hotel for the night."

"Why would I do that?"

"You want to be sure the combination of mushrooms and sleeping pills has time to kill Eric. If you go back too soon, you will have to call an ambulance. The last thing you want is for Eric to survive and deny he tried to kill himself."

"Okay, but how will I know the drugs will work?"

"The crushed mushroom alone will kill him. Adding sleeping pills is like putting extra chocolate on your ice cream. A blood test will easily confirm alcohol and sleeping pills. They won't even look for something as obscure as mushrooms. With the note, a finding of suicide is almost assured. Oh, and don't take any clothes or toiletries when you leave. Staying at the hotel has to look like a spontaneous decision."

"This scares me, Emily. I just don't know an easier way out."

"If you follow my plan, it will work out just fine. You must have the resolve to stick with your story."

"Okay," said Mary nervously.

"Do you have latex or rubber gloves?"

"Yes,"

"Good. Do not touch the computer or paper without the gloves on. After printing the note, take it into the bedroom and press Eric's hands and fingers all over it. You need to have his fingerprints on the note. Do the same with the pill bottle. Leave the bottle in the bedroom. Finally, place the note somewhere obvious. Before leaving, clean up any evidence that you were drinking with Eric. Take the gloves and mushroom pouch with you when you leave. Find a dumpster and dispose of the evidence. Do you understand these instructions?"

"Yes. I understand."

"Then, at least once while you are away, call Eric's cell phone. This will show you are concerned about him. Whoever you meet with, you must sell the story that Eric was drunk and threatening."

"That won't be hard. It's a regular part of my life," sighed Mary.

"I understand. You deserve better."

Emily used cash to pay for the breakfast, leaving a generous tip. "We never had this meeting. Understand?"

"Yes, I get it," replied Mary.

When Emily arrived home, she changed into tight navy blue yoga pants and a white Under Armour polyester V-neck shirt. She then drove to one of the Cactus View rec centers for her workout. Given her figure and physique, Emily enjoyed the men's looks as much as the exercise. She did her share of looking as well. Her routine included stretching, thirty minutes on a stationary bicycle, and finishing with the weight machines. After working up a good sweat, Emily drove back home. She walked into the house from the garage to find Bill sitting on the leather couch with a sullen look.

"What happened to you?" asked Emily.

"Did you see the paper today?" asked Bill.

"No, why?"

"There's a new article about Fred's accident. According to an unnamed source, the police suspect Fred was pushed off the trail."

"They already told you that, Bill."

"Yes, but I thought they were bluffing! Now it's in the paper. They think this was a homicide!"

"Bill, you need to control your emotions. If they had any evidence of homicide, we would have already been arrested."

"I don't care. This is freaking me out. I'm worried about the DNA."

"Stop this, Bill. They are bluffing."

"I'm not as secure with this as you are."

"Just let me handle it. You need to chill."

Bill scowled at Emily. "Don't tell me to chill. You told me there would be no suspicion over Fred's death. And now I'm reading in the paper the police think he was pushed. How would they know that?"

"Bill!" snapped Emily. "They are grasping. If they knew that, don't you think you would be arrested by now?"

"Me? What about you? It was your damn idea! It will be easy, you said. No one will suspect anything other than an accident, you said. You sucked me into it."

"Sucked you into it?" shouted Emily. "Were you sucked into screwing me while I was still married?"

Bill leaned over, putting his elbows on his knees while holding his head. "What are we going to do, Emily?"

Emily walked over and placed her left hand on Bill's shoulder. "Ignore it, Bill. You've talked to the police twice now. If they knew anything, we would have been arrested already. Go get yourself a drink. I need to take a shower."

Emily strolled to the master bathroom, started the shower, and pulled off her clothing. Stepping into the shower, Emily allowed the water to soak her head and flow over her body, hoping the warm water would soothe some of her anger with Bill. Emily reflected on her thoughts. *Why is Bill being so weak after showing such strength? I don't get it. His nervous behavior is a problem I did not expect from him. He may get us both arrested if he doesn't pull himself together soon. Bill is liable to sabotage our perfect accident. I can't let that happen.*

The bathroom door unexpectedly opened. Emily turned her head to look through the glass shower door. Bill was standing in front of her, naked.

"May I join you?" asked Bill.

Emily pulled back the glass door.

Bill stepped in, grabbed Emily, and pulled her close. "I'm sorry. I'm just nervous about this entire police investigation."

"It's going to be okay, Bill. Trust me."

After Mary arrived home, she was nervous. *What do I do with this mushroom powder until I need it? I can't let anyone find it.*

After looking around, Mary hid the pouch of mushroom powder in her underwear drawer. Eric would never go through her underwear. She placed the tiny coin pouch in the back of the drawer under multiple pairs of underwear. She then checked the liquor cabinet. A half bottle and an unopened bottle of bourbon were in the cabinet. Mary believed that would be more than enough. She then checked the medicine cabinet in the main bedroom for sleeping pills. Mary found a half-full bottle of pills. She hoped that would be enough. As she was reading the bottle, Mary heard Eric come into the house through the garage. She quickly replaced the bottle, shut the cabinet door, and hurried into the living room.

"What's wrong with you?" snapped Eric.

"Nothing. Why?" answered Mary nervously.

Eric gave Mary a strange look. "You look flustered or something."

"No, not at all. I ran some errands and just got home. How are you doing?"

"Me? I'm fine."

"Good," said Mary.

"I've been longing for a Freddy's double steakburger," said Eric. "Are you hungry?"

Mary wasn't, but she didn't want to say no to Eric. "Sure, I could go for something."

"Great, let's go."

Mary followed Eric out the door. She found it ironic that the man she was plotting to kill was taking her out to lunch. She wondered, *how many more times will we eat out together?*

Chapter 13

The following day, Ray Riggs arrived home at 11:45 a.m. after a morning of drop-in pickleball at the Cactus View courts. Linda was in the kitchen on her cell phone talking with Katy. "I don't know, Katy. Why don't you ask her?" After a pause, Linda said, "No, we're not going to discuss it in book club tomorrow. I need to go, Katy. I'll see you tomorrow night."

"What was that all about?" asked Ray.

"Oh, just Katy being Katy. She is still worried about the conversations from our last meeting. She also believes Emily is plotting something with Judy and Mary. Katy wants to bring it up at our book club meeting."

"I'd like to hear that conversation," said Ray. "Would you mind if I came to the meeting?"

"Only if you entertain Katy for the night."

Ray chuckled. "No, I think I'll pass on that offer."

"Katy keeps going on about Fred's accident not being an accident. There was an article in the paper saying there was evidence Fred may have been pushed off the mountain. Katy is also suspicious of the time Emily has been spending with Judy and Mary."

"What do you think of Emily?" asked Ray. "Is she all talk?"

"I don't know her all that well, but she doesn't come across as someone who would kill her husband. How does one ever know? She does think highly of herself."

"Some statements you told me Emily made might be of some concern."

"Yes, I agree," said Linda.

"Are you going to let Katy approach the subject?"

"No!" exclaimed Linda. "I told her it was inappropriate and none of her business."

"Smart move. In a related matter, Bill was not himself today," said Ray.

"Emily's boyfriend?"

"Yes. His mind was on something other than pickleball. He played about as poorly as I've seen from him."

"Did he say what was wrong?"

"I asked, but he brushed me off. Said everything was fine. But after hearing about this news article, I wonder if that was on his mind."

"I imagine it would be," said Linda.

"I'm going to shower," said Ray. "After I'm done, how about we go for lunch at State 48? We can sit outside and share a flight of beer samples with our meal. It will help clear our minds."

"I would like that," said Linda.

The following night was book club Wednesday. Except for Emily, everyone was present for the meeting by six o'clock. By the time everyone had gotten a drink and a plate of snacks,

Emily walked in at 6:20 p.m. She wore a red evening gown draped smoothly over her figure, and her light brown hair delicately framed her face. Dangling gold earrings hung from her ears.

"Well, good evening, ladies," announced Emily as she walked in. "It looks like the party has started."

"Why are you dressed like you're attending a formal reception?" asked Katy.

Emily looked at Katy and smiled. "Katy, my friend, this is not formal wear. Unlike some of us, I try to look my best when I go out."

Katy frowned and turned away.

"Well, you certainly look dashing," said Judy. "Come on in."

"What would you like to drink?" asked Linda.

"Do you have Merlot?"

"Always. Let me get you a glass. Help yourself to the food."

Mary walked over to Emily and whispered, "Thanks for coming." Emily nodded.

After some more casual conversation, Linda asked everyone to sit down to discuss Leslie Wolfe's book, The Girl From Silent Lake. "I hope everyone read it. Who would like to start?"

Sharon spoke up first. "Generally, I liked the story. Some parts were hard for me to read. Maybe it's my age."

"I don't think age has anything to do with it," said Maritza. "Some parts were tough for me to read as well. But the story is fantastic. I really liked the FBI Agent, Kay Sharp. And the profiling information was interesting. I never knew that even existed."

"I thought it was a splendid book," said Katy. "It really held my attention."

The discussion continued with members sharing what they liked or did not like about the story, the author's style, the story's setting, and so on.

"Mary," said Katy, "You haven't said anything about the book. What did you think?"

"I'm sorry, I just didn't have time to read it."

"Planning something, are we?"

"No. I've just been busy."

"Leave Mary alone," said Emily.

"I just asked a question," replied Katy. "I don't understand how a retired person wouldn't have time to read a book in four weeks."

"There could be many reasons," said Emily. "Mary is having a hard time with her husband right now."

"It doesn't matter," interrupted Linda. "Each of us has had lapses in reading from time to time. Now, are there any other comments about the book anyone wishes to share?"

No one else spoke up.

"Hearing none, casual hour may begin. Please help yourselves to more wine and snacks."

After several minutes, Katy noticed Emily, Judy, and Mary talking off to the side. She sauntered over to where they were standing. "Mary, I'm sorry to hear about your marital issues."

Mary sensed a lack of sincerity in Katy's voice. She smiled slightly and nodded her head.

"Do you plan on getting a divorce?" asked Katy.

"Katy, not now," said Emily.

"What? I'm just asking her a simple question. My husband, Jerry, is a financial manager. He might be willing to advise her on a financial strategy."

"We're still trying to work things out," said Mary. "But if I need someone, I'll keep Jerry in mind."

Katy then turned to Emily. "What was that article in the paper all about? Why do the police think your husband was pushed off the mountain?"

Emily's dark eyes glared at Katy. It was a sharp look that startled Katy.

"They don't think that, Katy. It's pure speculation by an unknown source. Do you think Fred was pushed?"

The tone of Emily's voice was not friendly.

"Me? How would I know," stammered Katy. "I just read the newspaper and wanted to know your thoughts."

Emily continued to stare at Katy. "Can you tell what my thoughts are now?"

Mary and Judy could feel the tension in the air. The conversation made Mary uncomfortable.

"I sense you don't like my question," said Katy.

"I don't like your insinuation that Fred's death was not an accident. It was ruled an accident three months ago."

"Apparently not," replied Katy. "Did you see the article?"

"Did you see it was from an anonymous source?"

"So what?"

"Anonymous sources are nothing more than gossip. Much like most of the crap that comes out of your mouth," said Emily sharply.

Several others in the room noticed the intense conversation between Katy and Emily. The room grew increasingly quiet.

"I talk no more crap than you do!" said Katy with a raised voice.

"Katy, you haven't liked me from the first time you saw me," replied Emily. "And in ten minutes, I picked you out as the club bitch."

"Did you just call me a bitch?" yelled Katy.

The room was now quiet, and all eyes were on Katy and Emily. With raised eyebrows, Emily flashed a sinister smile at Katy.

"Did you just call me a bitch?" repeated Katy.

"You are what you are, sweetie."

"You asshole," shouted Katy. "I know you killed your husband!"

Linda and Maritza quickly approached. Linda grabbed Katy by the arm, and Maritza stepped between Katy and Emily.

"That's enough!" shouted Linda. "The two of you are destroying this club. This is supposed to be a social, fun gathering of friends. I've about had it with both of you."

"It was until she joined," protested Katy.

"Katy, enough. We'll sort this out later. For now, I want both of you to leave."

Emily set her glass down. "I'm sorry if my presence upset anyone tonight." She then turned and walked out the door.

Linda looked at Katy. "You need to leave as well."

"Emily is the one who started getting all nasty with me."

"I don't care who started it. I won't stand for this type of behavior."

"Linda, you allowed a murderer in our club."

"You don't know that, Katy. Now please leave."

"Fine!" Katy set her half-consumed glass of chardonnay on a glass end table, then turned to the group. "Sorry if I upset anyone." She then walked out the door.

"What a hell of a mess that was," said Sharon. "Maybe we all need to read fairy tales."

"It was embarrassing," said Maritza.

"What was all the name-calling about?" asked Sharon.

"Oh, Katy is convinced Emily had something to do with her husband's death," replied Linda.

Sharon continued. "Mary, you seem to be close to Emily. What do you think? Has Emily confided in you?"

"All I know is that her husband slipped and fell."

"How about you, Judy?" asked Maritza.

"Same. All I know is what Emily has told me."

Linda interrupted. "Look, none of us knows for sure what happened. If it wasn't an accident, the police will figure it out. It's not our job to be judge and jury."

"Since Emily joined, the club hasn't been as enjoyable," Sharon reminded everyone. "I don't care for some of the conversations Emily has started. I'm getting too old for conflict."

"Katy started it," replied Judy. "She confronted Emily about the newspaper article. Anyone would have been offended."

"That's true," agreed Mary. "It felt like Katy was attacking Emily. God forbid one of your husbands dies. Katy may accuse you of murder. She can't seem to accept that accidents or illnesses happen."

Ray arrived home and walked into the living room, surprised that the club was still meeting.

"Late night, ladies?" asked Ray.

"You missed the fireworks," said Maritza. "Emily and Katy got into an argument."

"Oh, yeah?" replied Ray with an amused look.

"I'll explain it all later," said Linda. "Alright, everyone, that's enough for tonight. I will talk with Emily and Katy to let them know how we feel."

After everyone said their goodbyes and headed home, Ray asked Linda about the argument.

"Katy is still suspicious of Emily. Not only does she believe Emily may have pushed Fred off the mountain, but that she is planning something sinister with Mary and Judy."

"Sinister? Like what?" asked Ray.

"They both have poor marriages," said Linda. "Katy thinks they may be plotting to kill their husbands."

"Maybe I could see Judy doing that, but Mary? She seems too timid for anything like that."

"It's probably all in Katy's mind. However, Mary is miserable living with Eric."

"Then why doesn't she divorce him?"

"I've explained the control he has over their money."

"That's no reason not to get a divorce."

"Easy for you to say. Mary is terrified of Eric."

"Well, I'm going to bed. Are you coming?"

"Not yet. I need to decompress some, or I won't be able to sleep. Good night, Ray."

Chapter 14

The following morning, Mary met Judy at Judy's home after Jack left to play golf. As Judy made each of them a caramel latte, Mary asked about the fresh paint on half of Judy's house.

"Jack is painting our house. I tried to get him to hire someone, but he insisted he could do it and save money. He's sixty-one but still thinks he's thirty-one."

"How does he reach the peaks?"

"He has a big extension ladder."

Judy carried the lattes to the dining room table.

"You sounded stressed over the phone," said Judy.

"I can't get last night out of my mind. Katy knows what we're up to."

"Katy read that article and now thinks Emily must have killed Fred. I read it, and it sounded like the police were guessing."

"They don't believe it was an accident?" asked Mary.

"The article hinted it may not have been accidental."

Mary looked down. "That's what worries me."

"Why would it worry you, Mary?"

"I have some of the mushroom stuff Emily talked about," said Mary softly.

"Where did you get the mushrooms?"

"Emily."

"Emily gave you mushrooms?"

"Mushroom powder, to be precise."

"What are you planning, Mary?"

"A suicide."

"Oh my god, are you planning to kill yourself!?"

"No, no. Staging a suicide for Eric."

Judy sat back in her chair. "You're serious."

"Yes, I've had enough. I can't stand the man, and he controls everything. I need a way out."

"You took what Emily said seriously."

"I did. I've concluded there is no other way."

"Mary, you shouldn't be telling me this. Remember what Emily said."

"I have to talk to someone, Judy. I know I can trust you."

With her elbows on the table, Judy clasped her hands in front, leaned forward, and rested her chin on her hands. Several seconds of silence passed.

"Say something," pleaded Mary.

"Are you sure about this, Mary?"

"I don't see any other way out."

"Sorry, but I can't help you."

"I'm not asking for help. I just needed to talk to someone. I need your support, Judy. I'm going crazy."

"Okay, but don't give me any more information or details. Of course, I will support you. You're one of my best friends, and I know you've suffered. But you need to be careful. You could end up in prison."

"I've thought about that," responded Mary. "Truth be told, I've been in prison for a long time."

Judy nodded her head. "When is this going to happen?"

"It could be tonight or three months from now. Emily has coached me on the timing. It has to be a night..."

Judy held up her hand. "Stop. You're not supposed to talk about it. You've probably already said too much. Promise me you'll be careful."

"I will be. Promise."

Ray Riggs was home alone surfing the internet on his iPad when the doorbell rang. Ray walked to the door, opened it, and saw a black-haired male in a blue windbreaker standing on the porch. The man flashed a police badge and identified himself as Detective Lou Begay.

"Sorry to disturb you, Mr. Riggs, but I'd like to ask you a few questions about Fred Levine's death."

"Sure, detective, come on in."

Ray led Begay to the living room. "Have a seat anywhere."

Begay sat on the couch. Ray sat on a reclining chair facing Begay. "What can I answer for you?" asked Ray.

"I understand you are a friend of Bill Hutchins. Is that correct?"

"Somewhat. We don't socialize, but I occasionally play pickleball with him. His girlfriend is in my wife's book club."

"That would be Emily Settlemire, correct?"

"Yes."

"Do you know about Fred Levine's death? He was Emily's husband."

"Yes, I'm aware of that."

"Are you aware that Emily moved into Bill Hutchin's home soon after Fred's death?"

"I don't know when it was, but I know they live together."

"Has Bill ever talked to you about the accident?"

"He's told me Emily and Fred were hiking together when Fred slipped and fell."

"Do you believe him?"

"I don't have any reason not to."

"What about his affair with Emily?"

"Like I said, I only know they live together now."

"Has Emily said anything to you about it?"

"I haven't talked to Emily."

"What about your wife, Linda?"

"Yes, she's talked to her. They are friends through the book club."

"Is your wife here?"

"No. I believe she's out shopping."

"Has your wife said anything about Emily and her husband's death?"

"She's mentioned it. There was an article in the paper speculating the fall was not an accident. Is that what this is about?"

"We have evidence to indicate the fall was not accidental. We're trying to figure it out."

"I see," replied Ray.

"Here's my card," said Begay, handing Ray a blue business card. "Please have Linda call me when she gets home."

"Okay. I'll give Linda the message."

The discussion with Detective Begay had Ray concerned. He hadn't taken the murder talk too seriously but now believed there might be something to it. Ray had failed to tell the detective about Bill's strange behavior the last few days. He struggled to think Bill had participated in Fred's death. Ray tried to read a book while waiting for Linda to arrive home. However, he struggled to focus on what he was reading. Ray finally gave up, grabbed a Coors Light from the refrigerator, and retreated to the back patio to wait for Linda.

Ray was on his second beer by the time Linda arrived home. Linda walked onto the patio and observed the two beer cans on the small table next to Ray. Linda was surprised to see him drinking early in the day.

"You don't normally drink this early. Is everything okay?"

"I had a visit from Detective Begay with the Sheriff's department this morning. He was questioning me about Fred Levine's death."

"Why you?"

"I guess he knew we were pickleball friends. He wants you to call him."

Linda paused as a nervous sensation ran through her body. "He knows she's in my book club."

"Yes. He asked if you knew Emily, but I had the impression he already knew the answer."

"What am I going to tell him?" asked Linda.

"The truth."

"I know nothing about Fred's death."

"You've told me about the talk of arranged accidents and Mary wanting to be free from her husband. That might be valuable information."

"It was just talk, Ray. Mary couldn't do something like that. We get these ideas from all the books we read about betrayal and murder."

"I don't know, Linda. I had the impression the detective believed Fred was murdered."

"Emily has never admitted to anything other than it being an accident."

"An arranged accident," corrected Ray.

"She has hinted at it but never admitted it."

"Do what you think is right," said Ray.

"I will. I just don't know what that is right now."

Detective Begay was back at his desk when Detective Ashford approached him, holding a report in his hand.

"What have you got there?" asked Begay.

"Forensics just sent this over. It's the DNA analysis on Fred Levine's clothing."

Begay turned and grabbed the report. He quickly scanned the findings of the DNA testing. "This is hard to decipher."

"It is," said Ashford. "The analyst explained it this way. There are mixtures of DNA found on Fred's t-shirt. On the back of the shirt is a mixture of two, probably three, people. Some of the DNA is probably that of Emily Settlemire. It is the only female DNA on the shirt. The other DNA is a mixture of two males, one of which belongs to Fred Levine."

"That makes sense," said Begay. "Fred's sweat was probably all over the shirt. And it wouldn't be unusual for a wife's DNA to be on her husband's clothing. What about the third sample?"

"That is the unknown sample," replied Ashford.

"Is the lab sure the third sample is from a male?"

"Yes."

"Will they be able to compare it to Bill Hutchins?"

"Most likely."

"What do you mean by most likely?" asked Begay.

"Since it is a mixture, separating the distinct markers to positively identify the DNA is more difficult. But they believe they'll be able to do so."

"Where on the shirt was the mixture containing the third DNA located?" asked Begay.

"The right side of the upper back area."

"Bingo. Someone pushed Fred off that mountain."

"Maybe," replied Ashford.

"Why do you say that?"

"Someone may have innocently touched his back shoulder."

"What are you, a defense lawyer?"

"I'm just pointing out the issues."

"Yeah, I know. However, the pushing theory is supported, given the body's trajectory and where it landed. We need to find the owner of that DNA."

"Agreed," said Ashford.

"I'm going to pull Hutchins back in here and really put the pressure on him," stated Begay. He then picked up his phone and dialed Detective Dan Baxter.

"Hi, Lou. What's up?" answered Baxter.

"Your analysis of the crime scene just got stronger," said Begay.

"Oh yeah? Why?"

"The lab found a mixture of three DNAs on the back of Levine's shirt. One probably belongs to Emily Settlemire, one belongs to Levine, and the third is unknown. The DNA was on the upper back part of the shirt. Could be our killer."

"That would make sense," agreed Baxter. "Do you have any theory on who it might be?"

"My guess would be the new boyfriend, Bill Hutchins."

"I agree. But even if it turns out to be his, it doesn't prove he was on that mountain at the time of the fall."

"One issue at a time. I still need to talk to some women who may have more information, then I'm bringing Hutchins back in for some tough questions."

"Let me know if you need any help," said Baxter.

"I will. Thanks, Dan."

After Begay had gotten off the phone, Ashford spoke up. "Do you know if the White Tank Park has security cameras?"

Begay thought for a few seconds. "I'm not sure, but if they do, they would probably be at the entrances."

"If so," continued Ashford, "maybe one of the cameras caught Emily and her husband driving into the park. Depending on the angle, you might be able to tell if a third person was in the car."

"Excellent idea, Leland. Would you mind following up on that for me?"

"I'll get on it first thing tomorrow morning."

Begay got on the phone and called the number he had for Linda Riggs.

"Hello."

"Hello. This is Detective Lou Begay with the Maricopa Sheriff's Department. If you have some time, I'd like to visit with you on the Fred Levine case."

"Yes, my husband told me you wanted to talk to me. But I don't really know anything about it," said Linda.

"It only takes small bits of information to solve a case. If you are home, I can be there in twenty minutes."

"Well, okay. I'll be here."

Once she got off the phone, Linda swiftly walked to the garage where Ray was.

"Ray! Detective Begay just called me. He is coming over to talk to me."

Ray could see Linda was upset. "Calm down. It will be fine. He wants to find out what you know."

"But I know nothing."

"Just answer his questions truthfully, Linda."

Linda sighed and walked back into the house. She then called Maritza to explain what was happening.

"What should I tell him?" asked Linda.

"Just tell the truth."

"I don't know what the truth is. Many things were said in book club, but most were just talk. Should I tell him about the discussions we had?"

"I think most of it was conjecture of how women could end a marriage. No one admitted to anything," said Maritza.

"That's true," agreed Linda. "I have no proof that anything sinister happened."

As they were talking, the doorbell rang.

"Ooooh! He's here. I've got to go," said Linda.

Linda walked to the door and led Detective Begay to the dining room. They both sat at the table, and Begay introduced himself.

"You have a beautiful home, Mrs. Riggs."

"Thank you. You may call me Linda."

"Are you nervous, Linda?"

"No, why do you say that?"

"Your hand is shaking."

"Maybe a little," smiled Linda. "I've never been interviewed by the police before."

"You can relax. I don't think you had anything to do with Fred Levine's death."

"No, I certainly didn't!"

"I'm trying to determine what happened. You are a friend of Emily Settlemire, correct?"

"Yes."

"And I understand you manage a book club of women who meet regularly, correct?"

"Yes."

"Is Emily in the book club?"

"Yes."

"How long have you known Emily?"

"Not long. One of our members, Judy Kinderman, met Emily at an event or something. Judy liked her and found out she enjoyed reading crime novels. That is primarily what we read in our club, murder mysteries. Judy asked me if she could invite her, and of course, I said yes."

"Do you know Bill Hutchins?"

"Only through my husband. They play pickleball together."

"What has Emily told you about her husband's death?"

"Uh, not much. She said Fred died in a fall while hiking on White Tank Mountain."

"Did she say how he fell?"

"No."

"Have there been discussions at your book club about Fred's death?"

"Uh, what do you mean?"

"What did Emily tell people about his death?"

"Only that he fell."

"Was there any talk of it being an accident?"

"Yes, of course. It was, wasn't it?"

"We have evidence to believe Fred was pushed off the mountain."

"Oh dear. I didn't know that."

Begay could see Linda was uncomfortable. She kept pulling at her yellow blouse with a nervous tick.

"Were you aware Emily moved in with Bill Hutchins within weeks of Fred's death?"

"Not initially, but I later found out."

"Did that raise any suspicions about Emily?"

"I'm not sure."

"Not sure about what?"

"I didn't think about it."

"Did you think it was strange Emily would move in with another man within weeks of her husband supposedly having a tragic accident?"

"No, I mean, I don't know."

"What aren't you telling me, Linda?"

"There was some talk of husbands having accidents or something. I didn't really understand it all," exclaimed Linda.

"Who was talking about that?"

"Everyone. Excuse me, I need to get a glass of water. Do you want anything?"

"No, thank you."

Linda walked to the kitchen sink, filled a glass of water, and took a long drink. She filled the glass again, then walked back to the table.

"Are you okay?"

"Yes, I'm fine," Linda replied softly.

"What did Emily say about accidents?"

"I can't remember exactly. It was that sometimes husbands could have accidents or illnesses."

"Illnesses?"

"Yes, it was just general conversation about ways someone might lose a spouse."

"Did Emily say how these accidents or illnesses might happen?"

"What are you saying?" asked Linda.

"I'm asking you what Emily said."

"It was nothing specific. Just general conversation." Linda took another drink of water.

"What are you hiding, Linda?"

"Nothing! I know nothing but what I've told you."

"You appear to be very nervous," said Begay.

"I am. I've never been questioned by a detective before."

"Was Emily discussing ways to cover up murders of unwanted husbands?"

"Only in a general sense. I never heard any specific plans to murder anyone."

"But there was some discussion about it, correct?"

"Some, yes. It was not a serious conversation, Detective."

"Would other members of your club tell me the same thing?"

"I suppose. We talk about murder all the time. It's a book club focused on crime mysteries. That's all we talk about."

"Does it include how to cover up a crime?"

"NO! It's about the stories."

Ray walked in from the garage. "Is everything alright in here?"

"We're just finishing up, Mister Riggs," replied Begay. "Linda, I appreciate your cooperation. If you hear anything I should know, please call me."

Linda nodded.

"Do you have a list of all the book club members?"

"Yes. I'll get you a copy."

Linda walked into the den. Begay stood up. After a minute or two, she returned and handed Detective Begay a sheet of paper with the names and phone numbers.

"Thank you, Linda. Thank you, Mr. Riggs." Begay then turned and walked out the front door.

Linda collapsed in the chair and exhaled.

"What did he ask you?" asked Ray.

"His questioning was intense. I believe he knows something we don't."

"He should, Linda. He's the detective working on the case. It's obvious he believes Fred's fall was no accident."

"What do you believe?" asked Linda.

"I'm not sure, but ever since I found out Emily and Bill moved in together within weeks of the accident, I've had my suspicions."

"I need to call everyone to warn them. Detective Begay has all their names and numbers now."

"Maybe it's time to drop Emily from the club," said Ray. "From what you've told me, the club has been in turmoil since her arrival."

"Yeah, I suppose you're right."

Chapter 15

"Why do you keep lying to me!" Judy screamed at her husband, Jack.

"What are you bitching about now?" Jack responded.

"I saw you with Sherry again! You promised me it was over."

"Where did you see us?"

"At the Casa Café. You were sitting at a table in the back."

"Are you following me?"

"Just answer my question! Why are you still seeing her?"

"I'm not. We were just talking."

"You were having an affair with her, Jack! You promised it was over."

"You're overreacting. We're just friends."

"Friends, my ass. You can't stop, can you? What is wrong with me, Jack? Am I not pretty enough? Is the sex not good enough? What is it?"

Jack looked at Judy without responding.

"Tell me!" screamed Judy. "What is wrong with me?"

"Well, for one, you can be a real bitch, like right now."

"Huh? What do you expect? How many has it been, Jack? Three? Four? A dozen? You always have some excuse and promise me it's over. It's never over, is it?"

"We were just talking, Judy."

"You shouldn't even be near her! When did you last sit with me at the café to talk?"

"We don't talk. All you do is complain about my bad habits and things you don't like that I do."

"You mean, like screwing other women?"

"So now, if I'm talking to another woman, you think I'm screwing her?"

"You were having an affair with Sherry and promised it was over. Do you think I'm stupid? Where did you go from the café?"

"I ran some errands."

"Where? What did you buy?"

"See, this is what I hate. All the questioning."

"Do you know what I hate?" asked Judy.

Jack looked down.

"I hate you cheating on me and lying to me. I can't take it anymore."

"Then leave," snapped Jack.

"It's you who should leave. I don't want you here anymore."

Jack laughed. "After everything I've given you? You've had a tranquil life. My work allowed you to stay home to raise the kids. You never had to work in your life."

"Is that what you think? I would have loved a career. But I chose to stay home to raise our kids, to be there for them. I was there for them while you were building your career as a surgeon."

"I'm not leaving, Judy."

Judy let out a guttural scream. She then grabbed her car keys from the kitchen counter and stormed out the door. She drove her blue Honda Accord to Mary's house. Judy parked the car out front and sat for several minutes to calm herself. She then telephoned Mary.

"Hello?" answered Mary.

"Mary, it's Judy. Are you home?"

"Yes. Is everything okay?"

"No. I'm outside in my car. Do you mind if I come in?"

"Not at all."

Judy walked to the front door and was met by Mary. Mary could see that Judy had been crying.

"Come in," said Mary, as she led Judy to the living room. "Have a seat. Can I get you something?"

"A glass of water would be great," said Judy.

After retrieving two glasses of water, Mary sat down beside Judy.

"Tell me what's going on."

"Jack is still seeing that woman, Sherry."

"I'm sorry," said Mary.

"I really got angry with him and told him to leave. He refused," cried Judy.

"Take a few minutes to calm yourself."

Judy took two drinks of her iced water.

"I don't know what to do or where to go, but I can't live like this anymore."

"I would let you stay here, but the thing with Eric."

"Yeah, I know. I wouldn't ask you to do that. I could get a hotel room, but all my stuff is still at home."

"I can go back with you," said Mary.

Judy placed her face in her hands and gently cried.

Mary brushed back Judy's hair. "I've got enough of that mushroom powder if needed."

Judy lifted her head and sighed. "I've actually given that some thought, but it's not something I can do."

"I understand. I just wanted to make the offer. Do you want to get some of your clothes and things from the house?"

"Yes, I would like that."

"Alright, let me leave a message for Eric. I'll say I'm running to Walmart. Then we can go."

"Thank you, Mary."

When Judy and Mary returned to the house, Jack was painting the outside walls. It was a project he had been working on for several days. Judy and Mary entered the house while saying nothing to Jack. After Judy had packed a bag with some clothing and toiletries, both left the house and walked toward Judy's car. Jack noticed Judy was carrying a small suitcase.

"Where are you going?" shouted Jack.

"Anywhere but here," shouted Judy.

"If you leave, don't you ever return!" yelled Jack.

"Go to hell!" screamed Judy as she walked to her car.

Jack didn't reply.

After returning to Mary's home, Mary assisted Judy in getting a room at the local Hampton Inn. Before Judy could leave, Mary's husband, Eric, walked into the house and stopped at the refrigerator to grab a beer. He then saw Judy with her red suitcase.

"What's going on?" asked Eric.

"Nothing," said Mary. "Judy and I were just visiting."

"Then what's the suitcase for?"

"Uh, I'm visiting a friend for the night," said Judy.

Eric took a swig of beer. "What's Jack doing?"

"He's painting the house."

"Well, a good time to get away, I suppose."

"You should get going," said Mary.

"Thank you again," said Judy before leaving the house.

Linda's phone buzzed. It was Sharon calling. "Hello, Sharon."

"I just had a detective at my house asking me many questions about Emily and our book club. What's going on?"

"The police are still investigating Fred's death."

"Yeah, but he asked about things Emily may have said."

"The detective talked to me as well," said Linda.

"He believes Fred's fall was no accident," said Sharon.

"How did you respond to that?" asked Linda.

"Well, I told him I didn't know what happened to Fred. He kept asking questions about things said during our book club meetings."

"What did you say about our book club?" asked Linda.

"I told him I left when the conversation turned to the talk of murder. Are we all being investigated because of Emily?"

"We are not under investigation, Sharon. This is what the police do when they suspect something is amiss. They ask lots of questions of friends, relatives, and co-workers. It's part of the investigation."

"This book club is becoming too intense for me," said Sharon. "I may not come back."

"Please don't quit, Sharon. You are a valuable member of our group. I will let Emily know that until this investigation ends, she must stay away."

The following day was the last Saturday in February. It was a warm day, even by Arizona standards. It was 4:30 p.m. when Mary arrived home from grocery shopping. Eric was sprawled on the sofa watching a college basketball game between Arizona State and Oklahoma. Mary noticed Eric was drinking a bourbon and coke on ice.

"Hey, Mary, when you finish putting those groceries away, would you make me another bourbon?"

"I'll be happy to, Eric."

Mary quickly put up the groceries and then walked to the bedroom. She reached into her underwear drawer to retrieve the small red pouch containing the mushroom powder. She also grabbed a small pill bottle into which she had emptied the powder from twenty-one sleeping pills. Mary then returned to the kitchen to make Eric his bourbon and coke. She grabbed a drinking glass and filled it halfway with ice. She then filled two-thirds of the glass with bourbon and topped it off with coke. Mary then put some sleeping powder into the drink and stirred it. Mary hoped it would help make Eric drowsy. She then sprinkled just a tiny amount of mushroom into the drink.

Mary walked into the living room to hand Eric his drink.

"You didn't have to get me a fresh glass," said Eric.

"Eh, it was right there, so I used a clean one. Let me know when you need a refill."

Eric gave Mary a puzzled look. "Why are you being so nice? Do you want something?"

"No. I'm just trying to be a better wife."

Eric smiled. "Well, so far, so good."

Mary left Eric to watch the game while she sat in the dining room and pretended to be reading a book. All she could think about was whether her plan would work. Mary monitored the level of Eric's drink, ready to refill it as needed. Once she saw his glass almost empty, Mary walked over to retrieve the glass.

"I'll get you another one," said Mary as she grabbed the glass from the end table.

"Not quite as strong," said Eric. "I'm already feeling a bit woozy."

"Okay," replied Mary.

Mary mixed up another bourbon and coke, holding back on some of the bourbon. This time, she did not add sleeping powder, only a bit of mushroom powder. Mary was afraid it would put him to sleep before the hefty dose. After giving Eric the second drink, she watched closely. It was clear to Mary that Eric was intoxicated. How much was attributed to the sleeping pills and mushroom powder was unknown.

After another thirty minutes had passed, the basketball game was over. Eric flipped through the TV channels, looking for something else to watch. This was Mary's opportunity. She walked into the living room.

"Eric, if you come to the bedroom with me, I'll fix us both another bourbon and make it worth your time."

"What do you mean?" asked Eric.

"I'll do whatever you want tonight. I'm in a sexy mood."

Eric was surprised by Mary's suggestion. It was not like her. The effects of the alcohol and drugs were making it difficult for Eric to focus.

"You're different tonight. But I like it."

"Is that a yes?"

"It's a hell yes. I won't say no to an offer like that."

"You go into the bedroom and get comfortable. I'll make us some drinks."

Eric stood up, grabbed the arm of the couch to steady himself, and then walked to the bedroom.

Mary went to the kitchen counter to mix the drinks. This time, she used an oversized glass, afraid Eric might taste the mushroom powder in a regular drink glass. Mary only put a small amount of bourbon in her glass. In Eric's glass, she put a large amount of bourbon, the remainder of the sleeping powder, and a teaspoon of the mushroom powder, just as Emily had suggested.

When Mary entered the bedroom, Eric had removed his clothing and was lying on the bed. Mary walked over and handed Eric his drink.

"Why the big glass?" asked Eric.

"I didn't want to have to leave the bed once I got here."

"Good thinking," Eric slurred. "Now, why don't you climb up on top of me?"

"Not yet," replied Mary. "We are going to have a little party. When was the last time we drank together in celebration? Don't worry; your night will end with a big surprise."

Mary held up her glass and shouted, "Cheers!" She then took a big gulp from her drink.

Eric did likewise.

"Do you remember when we first married?" asked Mary.

"Sure, why?"

"We had so much fun together. This is the start of a new era for us."

Eric gave a half smile. He was feeling a little nauseous.

"Drink up!" said Mary. "Once you finish that drink, I will do whatever you want."

By this time, Eric was feeling quite buzzed. Eric took several large drinks from his glass. Mary did the same.

"I'll bet I can chug the rest of mine before you do," said Mary. She could see Eric was now very intoxicated.

Eric slurred, "like hell you can."

"Ready?" asked Mary. "Go!"

Eric raised his glass and started to slurp it down. Mary raised her drink but only pretended to be gulping it. Once Eric was finished, he fell back onto his pillow. His breathing was shallow.

"Are you okay, Eric?"

"Yeah, just give me a minute. That whiskey hit me hard."

After a few minutes, Mary could see Eric was in some distress.

"Is everything okay, Eric?"

"I don't know," said Eric. "My stomach doesn't feel so good, and I'm getting a cramp in my upper right chest."

Mary knew the liver was in the upper right chest cavity. She figured some of the mushroom powder had reached the liver through the bloodstream. As Mary watched, Eric's breathing became more rapid and shallow. She continued to watch him. Sweat was forming on his brow, and he could barely keep his eyes open.

"Eric, you don't look so good."

"Yeah," panted Eric. "I'm not feeling so good either."

"What's wrong?"

"My side hurts, and my eyes can't focus."

Eric's speech was sloppy. Mary had to listen carefully to what he was saying. Then Eric's eyes appeared to roll back, and his eyelids closed.

Mary continued to monitor Eric's condition, hoping she had given him enough poison to do the trick. If he lived, she knew he would likely kill her.

After a half hour, Eric was still breathing. Several times, Eric had writhed in pain without waking up. Mary guessed it must be the mushrooms doing their magic. Mary picked up her glass, took it to the kitchen, and washed it. She then put it back into the cupboard. When Mary returned to the bedroom, she noticed a milky substance had run from Eric's mouth and down the side of his left cheek. It looked like vomit. Eric was in a spasm, gasping for air. Mary could no longer watch. She had to leave the room.

Mary sat in the living room and cried. Even though she hated Eric for his abuse, it was still difficult to see him suffer in this manner. *What have I done? Have I just taken Eric's life and sentenced myself to life in prison?*

After another half hour, Mary composed herself and went to the bedroom again. Eric was splayed out naked on the bed, his mouth open, eyes shut, and with no movement or sounds of breathing. His face was white. Mary panicked. She took a few deep breaths and tried to remember what Emily had told her. She went through the steps in her head.

Mary retrieved a pair of nylon gloves and put them on. She then went into Eric's office, got on his computer, and wrote out the following note:

Dear Mary,

I'm so sorry to leave you this way. I cannot live without you. Forgive me for ever hurting you. Please tell the kids I love them – Eric.

Mary then printed out the note. With her hands shaking, she then carried the note into the bedroom. As Emily instructed, Mary pressed the note against Eric's hands. As she was doing this, tears blurred her vision. She returned the note to Eric's office and set it on his desk. Mary then retrieved the sleeping pill bottle and tossed it on the bed. After that, Mary placed the nearly empty bottle of bourbon on the table next to Eric's side of the bed. She then took Eric's glass back to the kitchen. There, she wiped down the glass to remove her fingerprints. Mary carried the glass back to the bedroom and carefully pressed Eric's fingers onto the glass.

After being satisfied with the crime scene setting, Mary took the pouch containing the mushroom powder and nylon gloves and put them into a paper bag. She looked around one last time. Satisfied there was nothing left to do, Mary grabbed her keys and left the house. She drove to a nearby Fry's supermarket parking lot. After parking, Mary sat in the car shaking for twenty minutes. Mary tried to calm herself down. Once she had stopped crying, Mary called Linda Riggs.

When Linda answered, she could immediately tell something was wrong. "What is it, Mary?"

"I've left Eric."

"Left him? For good?"

"Yes. I told Eric I couldn't live with his abuse anymore, and I was leaving him. I'm filing for a divorce."

"Where are you right now?"

"I'm sitting in a parking lot. I don't know where to go, but I can't return home to Eric. I'm afraid of what he might do to me."

"Come to our house," said Linda. "You can stay here until you find a place to live."

"No, I can go to a hotel somewhere."

"Nonsense. Come over right now."

"Are you sure?"

"Yes. We have an extra bedroom. It will give you time to find another place to live."

"Thank you so much, Linda."

Chapter 16

Mary hardly slept through the night. She fretted all night over her poisoning of Eric. Had she done the right thing? Would the police believe it was suicide? Did she cover her tracks well enough? What would prison be like?

Once Mary heard someone rustling around in the kitchen, she got up, put on a bathrobe, and walked out. Linda was making coffee.

"Good morning, Mary," said Linda. "Did you sleep well?"

"Not much. I kept thinking about this divorce and how Eric might react."

"I'm sure he'll be angry, but you needed to leave him. Your next step will be to find an excellent attorney."

"It's all so messy. Eric has hidden most of the money."

"Don't worry about that now. The priority is your safety. I'm sure one of your kids will help you."

"I suppose," agreed Mary. "My first priority will be returning to Minnesota to help my elderly mother. After that, who knows?"

"Would you like some breakfast?"

"No, thank you. I'm not hungry. I think I'll go take a shower and get dressed."

Once Mary returned to the guest bedroom, she remembered Emily had instructed her to call Eric's phone. Mary used her cell phone to call Eric. She allowed the phone to ring until it went to voice message.

"Eric, I just wanted to let you know I'll be home in a few days to pick up more of my things. Let me know when it's a good time to come."

Mary sat on the edge of the bed, looking down at her hands. They were both shaking. She took several deep breaths to calm her nerves, then went into the guest bathroom for her shower. As the warm water ran across Mary's bare skin, it felt like her emotions were being swept away for a few minutes. She closed her eyes and imagined a life without Eric. However, as much as Mary tried, she could not wash out the thoughts of prison that kept popping up in her head.

Once Mary was dressed for the day, she called Judy to arrange a meeting at the café. Mary then returned to the kitchen, where Linda and Ray had just finished breakfast.

"Are you ready for something to eat?" asked Linda.

"No, thank you. I have some errands to run."

"Will you be back for dinner?"

"That would be nice. Thank you."

"Okay. We'll see you then."

After Mary had left, Ray commented, "She didn't look so well."

"No. I'm worried about her. She doesn't have access to money, and Eric is vengeful. He will fight her all the way."

When Mary arrived at the café, Judy was already seated at a table with two coffees in front of her.

"Hi Mary, what's going on?"

"We can't talk here. Is there somewhere more private we can talk?"

"Let's see. Sure, how about the library? They have a couple of private reading rooms. We can see if one of those is available."

Mary and Judy walked from the café to the library. Fortunately, one room was vacant. They walked in and shut the door.

Mary began to cry. Judy put her arm around Mary's shoulder. "What is it, Mary?"

"It's done," cried Mary.

"What's done?"

"Eric's dead."

Judy was stunned. "What happened?"

"He committed suicide," answered Mary while wiping tears from her cheeks.

Judy's mouth dropped open. She recalled their conversations and was at a loss for words.

After several uncomfortable seconds, Mary said, "Say something, Judy."

"I don't know what to say. Did you...?"

"Don't ask me that," interrupted Mary. "He committed suicide, Judy."

"Okay. How did Eric commit suicide?"

"I believe the police will determine it was alcohol and sleeping pills."

"Have the police questioned you?"

"You're the only one who knows right now."

Judy sat back in her chair. "Are you saying the police haven't been notified?"

"No."

"You haven't called them?"

"No. I haven't found the body yet."

"Okay, I'm confused," said Judy.

"I left Eric. I told him I was filing for divorce and spent the night at Linda's."

"But you know he committed suicide, right?"

"I believe that's what the police will find."

Judy nodded. "I get it. You're following Emily's script. Be vague, and don't admit to anything. I will not ask you any more questions. What do you need from me?"

"I just need your support and understanding."

"I'm here for you, Mary. But you shouldn't have told me this before the police found the body."

"I know," said Mary. "But I had to talk to someone. I couldn't tell Linda. She wouldn't understand the way you do. It felt like I had a thousand bees buzzing in my gut. I just had to talk to someone. I won't even mention I came to you."

"Are you sure he's dead?" asked Judy.

"I couldn't detect any breathing, and he had vomit coming out of his mouth."

Judy nodded. "Sounds like he was dead."

"Does Jack know you were meeting me this morning?" asked Mary.

"No. I haven't talked to him since Friday."

"Good. I don't want anyone to know we met this morning."

"I won't tell anyone," Judy assured her.

"How's your room at the Hampton Inn?" asked Mary.

"It's fine. Better than being home with that cheating asshole. If you want to join me, the room has two king beds."

"I don't think that would be wise right now," said Mary. "We probably shouldn't be seen together for a couple of days. It might raise some questions."

"I suppose you're right," agreed Judy.

Once they were finished talking, Judy left the library first. After a few minutes, Mary left.

Mary spent the next several hours meandering about town. She wanted to be seen and recorded on video at several places to build an alibi. She stopped at Walmart to purchase some toiletries, Fry's Supermarket for a twelve-pack Diet Coke, and then at a QT convenience store to fill her car with gas. They were all places Mary knew had video surveillance. She believed this would help build her alibi. Mary returned to Linda and Ray's home at 3:15 p.m.. Mary made another phone call to Eric in front of Linda and Ray. Again, she left a message saying she would return the next day to pick up some clothing and personal items.

The next morning, the first day of March, was not as warm as the previous day. A swirling wind made it feel even cooler. It was 9:30 a.m. when Emily and Bill heard a knock on the front door. Emily answered it. On the porch stood Detectives Begay and Ashford.

"Now what?" asked Emily.

"Is Bill Hutchins here?" asked Begay.

"Yeah."

"We'd like to speak with him."

"Who's at the door?" Bill yelled from inside the house.

"It's Detectives Begay and Ashford," shouted Begay. "We need to speak with you, Bill."

Bill walked to the front door. "What's this about now?"

"We have some more questions to ask you, Bill. Just a few details we need to resolve."

Bill was hesitant. "What questions do you have?"

"We would prefer to do this at the Sheriff's Department," said Begay.

"Are you arresting me for something?"

"No. We have some additional information to ask you about. It's better if we do it at the station."

"I don't want to go to the station. You can ask me questions here."

Begay and Ashford looked at each other. "Can we come in?" asked Begay.

"No, you're not coming in," interrupted Emily. "I've answered your questions, and so has Bill. Go work on some actual crime."

"We have additional evidence. You don't want to know what it is?" asked Begay.

The words "additional evidence" felt like a lightning bolt shooting through Bill's chest. He had to know what they knew.

"Let them in," said Bill. "I'll answer their questions. I have nothing to hide."

Both detectives sensed a nervousness in Bill's voice.

Bill directed them to the dining room table. The detectives sat across from Bill. Emily sat to the right of Bill.

"We would like to speak to Bill alone," said Begay.

"No, she can stay," said Bill. "We have nothing to hide."

Bill's words were not in sync with his body language. The deep breath, the licking of his lips, and the tapping of his right foot on the floor were all signals to the detectives. It was not the look of a man with nothing to hide.

"We want to be sure we understand your previous statements," said Begay. "You have told us you were not hiking with Emily and Fred. Is that still your contention?"

"We've already been through this!" shouted Emily. "Are you going to keep asking the same questions over and over until you get an answer you like?"

"Well, certainly an answer we believe to be the truth."

"We've told the truth. If all you want to do is ask the same questions, then this interview is over."

"Excuse me, but are you an attorney?" asked Begay.

"No."

"Well, we have some information I think Bill would be interested in." Begay then looked directly at Bill. "We've done DNA testing on Fred's clothing. Would you like to know what we found?"

"Yes," nodded Bill nervously.

"They are just baiting you, Bill," said Emily.

"Maybe we should just go get a warrant," said Ashford.

"No, no," replied Bill. "Emily, just shut up for now. I want to hear what the detectives have."

"We found both male and female DNA on the back of Fred Levine's shirt," said Begay. "Do you suppose the male DNA is yours?"

"What does that mean?" asked Bill.

"It means we have additional evidence Fred was pushed off that mountain. Is that DNA yours, Bill?"

"No. It's not mine. I wasn't with Emily that day."

"You mean Emily and Fred, right?"

"Yes, yes, of course. Emily and Fred."

"So, when we compare this DNA to yours, it will not match, correct?"

Ashford could see the pace of Bill's foot tapping had increased. Bill was also rubbing his hands together.

"No, it can't be mine," said Bill.

"Is that all, detectives?" asked Emily.

"No," said Begay. "We need DNA samples from you and Bill."

"He's not giving you any DNA sample," shouted Emily. "This is a witch hunt. You can leave now."

Begay frowned at Emily. He wanted to arrest her right then and there. "Okay, we can leave. But we'll return later this afternoon with a court order to take your DNA sample. At that point, we will drag your asses back to the department to extract the samples. Or, we can take a swab of your mouth right now and then leave. Which is it going to be?"

"Get out," said Emily.

"No, Emily," said Bill in a raised voice. He then looked at Begay. "Take your sample, and then leave us alone."

Ashford pulled out an envelope from his inside jacket pocket. He pulled out two long cotton swabs, then swabbed Bill's left inside cheek with both swabs. He replaced them in the envelope, sealed them, and labeled them.

"Now we need your DNA, Emily," said Begay.

"My DNA was all over Fred. I was his wife."

"Yes, and we must confirm the female DNA is yours."

Reluctantly, Emily allowed Ashford to perform the same collection process on her.

"We're done," said Ashford.

"Oh, one more thing," said Begay. "Will camera footage of cars entering the parking lot at White Tank show you in the car, Bill?"

"I wasn't in the car," responded Bill.

Begay nodded. "Okay, well, thank you for your time. And thank you, Emily, for your hospitality."

Emily smirked.

Both detectives then stood and left the house.

Once they were gone, Bill turned toward Emily. "What am I going to do now?"

"Stop worrying," said Emily. "You hardly touched Fred."

"Easy for you to say. You can explain your DNA. They also have videos of cars entering the park. What if they see me driving in?"

"They are looking for one of our cars, not yours. The detective asked if you would be seen in our car. You weren't in our car."

Bill rubbed his forehead. "Damn it! I should never have gone along with this plan. Why didn't you just divorce the man?"

"Don't act like you don't know. My worth is now over five million. No one turns that kind of money down. You wouldn't be driving that new BMW without my money. And best of all, you now sleep with me every night guilt-free."

"I can't say I'm guilt-free right now."

Emily was concerned Bill would crack if brought in for another interview. She believed Bill's DNA could be explained away, but Bill was not up to it.

"It's going to be alright, Bill. Trust me."

"I need to take a walk to think alone," said Bill. "My mind is racing right now. I'll see you when I get back."

After Bill had left, Emily stewed over what to do about Bill. She thought being a firefighter would have made him emotionally strong enough to handle the pressure. Emily now knew she had been wrong. While she loved Bill, Emily loved her freedom and money even more. Emily paced the house, worrying Bill's weakness would destroy their lives. There was only one thing Emily could do to ensure her freedom. Emily picked up her cell phone and dialed a number.

"Yeah, Chris here," answered Chris Molina.

"Chris, it's Emily. We need to meet soon. I've got a job for you."

"Damn, I didn't expect to hear from you. You got the fifty grand?"

"Yeah, I got it. Can you meet with me tomorrow?"

"Where at?"

"Do you know where Stonebrook Park is? It's off West Ely Drive. I can be there around two o'clock."

"I can find it."

"Great. I'll be on the south end wearing a white wide-brimmed floppy hat and dark sunglasses."

"Yeah, I'll find ya. I'll need half the money upfront."

"I understand. See you tomorrow."

Mary and Linda had spent most of the morning discussing Mary's marital situation. After another cup of coffee, Mary told Linda she needed to return home to pack more of her things. She also wanted Linda as a witness when Mary discovered Eric's body.

"I hate to ask, but I'm afraid to return to the house alone," said Mary. "Who knows what Eric might do?"

"I completely understand. I'll happily go with you."

Linda accompanied Mary as she drove home. Mary pulled into the driveway, shut off the car, and then used her remote to open the garage door. Eric's car was in the garage. Mary hesitated.

"What's wrong?" asked Linda.

"I didn't think he would be home," replied Mary.

"I'm with you, and I have my cell phone. If Eric gives you any trouble, I will immediately call the police."

"Okay. Thank you."

Mary and Linda walked to the front door. The house looked and sounded quiet. Mary opened the door and stepped inside. Nothing was on. No TV, no lights, nothing. Linda detected an unpleasant odor.

"What's that smell?" asked Linda.

"I'm not sure."

Mary walked through the kitchen, calling out Eric's name. "Eric, are you home? Eric, where are you?"

She continued down the short hallway toward the master bedroom. Linda was close behind. Mary pushed open the bedroom door and immediately let out a blood-curdling scream.

"Oh, my god!" screamed Mary. "Oh, my god!"

Mary rushed to the bedside, screaming hysterically. Linda followed her in and was shocked to see Eric sprawled out on the bed naked. An odor of decay filled the room, much stronger than in the living room. Linda could see dried fluid on Eric's left cheek and on the bedsheet. His body looked pale and bloated. An empty drink glass and an almost empty bottle of bourbon sat on the table next to the bed.

"Linda, Eric's dead!" cried out Mary.

"I can see that. It looks like he drank himself to death. There's also a pill bottle on the bed," said Linda as she covered her mouth and nose with a handkerchief.

"Let's get out of here," said Linda. "We need to call the police."

Linda grabbed Mary by the arm and led her out of the room. She continued to lead her until they were back outside.

Mary forced herself to cry. She hoped her dramatics were convincing while Linda called 911. Mary could hear her talking with the dispatcher. Within minutes, Mary heard sirens growing louder as they approached the Cactus View neighborhood.

After arriving and conducting a preliminary search of the house, one of the uniformed officers took statements from Mary and Linda. Other officers secured the crime scene.

Within thirty minutes, a crime scene van had arrived. Two crime scene investigators (CSIs) entered the house with large briefcases. One of them was carrying a camera.

After an officer obtained a complete statement from Linda, she was free to leave.

"I'd like to stay with my friend."

"You could, but it will be a while. We have a detective coming who will want to interview her."

"That's fine. I'll wait. Do we have to be in a police car?"

"I'm afraid so. This is a potential crime scene now. We don't want anyone contaminating it," said the officer.

Ten minutes later, an official-looking fortyish white male with thinning blond hair and a mustache walked across the rocked front yard. Linda assumed it was the detective. He was wearing a gray sports jacket and dark slacks. He stopped to talk with two officers on the front porch. After several minutes, the detective walked through the front door. Twenty minutes later, he walked back out. Linda saw an officer pointing toward the patrol car she and Mary were sitting in. The detective walked to the vehicle and leaned down toward the open window.

"Good morning. I'm Detective Dan Baxter with the Surprise Police Department. You must be Linda?"

"Yes," responded Linda.

"And you must be Mary?"

Mary nodded, "Yes."

"Linda, I need to talk to Mary alone. You are free to go, or you can wait in the car here. It could take some time."

"Go on, Linda. I'll be fine."

"Are you sure?"

"Yes. I appreciate your help. I'll see you back at your place."

Once Linda had left, Detective Baxter took Mary to his car. He allowed her to sit up front. After exchanging some pleasantries, Baxter got to work.

"Tell me what happened this morning."

"I was staying with my friend Linda. I had told my husband I was leaving him. I last saw him Saturday night. I tried calling him to schedule a time to get my things, but he wouldn't answer. Today, Linda and I came over, and that's when I found Eric."

"When was the last time you saw Eric alive?"

"Saturday night, around seven. That's when I left."

"What was his condition?"

"Eric was drinking heavily, which isn't that unusual. He was upset after I told him I was filing for a divorce."

"Is that why you left Saturday night?"

"Yes."

"Why were you wanting a divorce?"

"Eric was an abuser. It wasn't bad initially, but it got worse over time. I finally had enough. I decided to leave him."

"What was his reaction when you told him?"

"Eric was angry. He was also heartbroken. We'd been married almost forty years."

"Did he abuse you Saturday night?"

"He threatened me. That's when I left."

"How did he threaten you?"

"He threatened to kill me."

"Has he ever physically assaulted you?"

"Many times."

"Did you ever call the police?"

"I did once in Minnesota."

"Was he arrested?"

"Yes, but they let him go the next day. I think he got a deferred sentence after a treatment plan."

"You never called the police any other time?"

"I was afraid to. Eric threatened to beat me silly and take our kids away. I couldn't risk that," explained Mary. "He once told me he would kill me and bury me under concrete."

"When did he threaten to kill you?" asked Baxter.

"It was years ago in Minnesota after I had called the police. I never called them again."

"I'm sorry to hear that," said Baxter. "Was Eric alive when you left on Saturday?"

"Huh?"

"I asked if Eric was alive when you left on Saturday."

"Yes. Of course."

"I could see why you might want Eric dead."

"No. I just wanted a divorce. That's what I told him."

"Can you explain the sleeping pills to me?"

"Those were Eric's. Sometimes, he had trouble getting to sleep."

"Was he taking the pills while you were home?"

"No."

"Had Eric ever threatened suicide before?"

"A few times. I had threatened to leave on past occasions. Whenever I did, he would get upset. He would tell me he would rather die than live without me. I never believed it until now."

"Mary, we found Eric in bed, naked. Was Eric in bed when you left?"

"No. He was in the living room."

"Was he naked?"

"No."

"Why do you think he took his clothes off?"

"Uh, sometimes he would get hot and sleep in the nude."

"Is there anything else you want to tell me, Mary?"

"Not that I can think of."

"I'm sorry for putting you through this. We'll talk again. You are free to leave. Do you need a ride?"

"No, I have my car."

Chapter 17

By mid-morning on Tuesday, everyone in the book club had heard about Eric. Linda had talked to everyone in trying to contain the rumors. In addition to the news of Eric's death, Detective Begay had called the list of club members to interview each member about what she knew about Emily Settlemire and Fred's death. The rumors were spreading beyond the club. Friends were calling club members to determine if the rumors were true.

After Judy's interview with Detective Begay, she met Mary at the Casa Café in the community square. After getting coffee and muffins, they sat outside at a round table shaded by a tree.

"Are you okay, Mary?" asked Judy.

"I'm a nervous wreck. But each day gets a little easier."

"I would say I'm sorry for your loss, but I'm not sure that's appropriate. You are better off without Eric."

"I'm no longer afraid of being abused. Now I'm just praying the police determine Eric died by suicide."

"It was a suicide, correct?" asked Judy.

"Yes, of course."

"Are you still okay with the decisions you've made?"

"I had no choice but to leave Eric. I feel safer now."

"I envy you, Mary. You're free while I'm still married to a cheating scumbag."

"I'm sorry, Judy."

"Don't be. I should have left Jack a long time ago. If I had the guts, I'd eliminate Jack from my life."

Mary wasn't sure how to respond.

"That detective came to see me," said Judy.

"Which detective?" asked Mary.

"Detective Begay."

Mary breathed a sigh of relief. "You scared me. I thought it might have been the Surprise detective. What did he ask you about?"

"He wanted to know what Emily said about how Fred had died. I told him I didn't know how Fred died. I only knew what Emily had told us, that he had accidentally fallen. However, then he asked if there had been discussions at our book club about how to kill people. He brought up some things Katy had told him. I just brushed it off by saying it was all part of our discussion on the books we've read."

"Did he believe you?"

"I'm not sure."

"I wish Katy would just shut up," replied Mary. "Those were private, hypothetical discussions among friends."

"Katy has a big mouth," agreed Judy.

Mary looked at the clock on her iPhone. "I need to get going. I'm meeting with an attorney this afternoon to review Eric's estate. He's going to help me fight for my home and Eric's money. What do you have planned?"

"I'm going back to the house to get more of my things and then look for a more permanent place to live," said Judy.

"Good luck, Judy."

Judy watched as Mary walked away. She couldn't stop pondering how Mary had been so brave in escaping her situation. Truth be told, Judy was jealous of Mary finally being free of her husband.

Jack had already called Judy several times, demanding that she return to the house, promising he would end his affair. It was a scenario that had been played out multiple times. Judy wanted no more of it. However, she knew a divorce battle would be fierce. As a surgeon, Jack made the money for the family. Judy's highest-paid job had been as a Kohl's department store manager. Even if Judy won a large settlement, she believed Jack would avoid paying. He had once threatened to leave the country if she tried to take his money.

Judy drove from the community center to her home. The garage door was open, and Jack's car was in the garage. Judy parked on the street and walked toward the garage. Judy heard some noise coming from the backyard. She walked along the side of the house to the back patio. Jack was on an aluminum extension ladder approximately fourteen feet up from the concrete patio. Judy could see he was painting the top trim on the roof peak.

Judy called up to Jack. "I'm getting some clothes and personal items out of the house."

Jack looked down from the ladder. "Where the hell have you been? I've been calling you."

"Yeah, I didn't want to talk to you anymore. We're done, Jack. I'm just going to get some things, and then I'll be out of here."

"Not while I'm up here. You wait until I finish. We need to talk, and I don't want you rummaging through my house."

"It's my house, too, Jack."

"Not anymore. You left, remember?"

"How can you be serious!" screamed Judy. "How many affairs have you had, Jack? Four? Twelve?"

"Shut the hell up!" shouted Jack. "You'll disturb the neighbors."

"I don't care who hears me!" shouted Judy. "You've been a cheating jackass of a husband for too long. I'm not putting up with it anymore."

"Maybe if you weren't such a bitch, I wouldn't have cheated," yelled Jack.

Judy's anger was growing to a fever pitch. How could Jack try to blame her for his cheating? Judy's mind was racing. Jack blaming her, and the thought of fighting Jack over everything for the next year or more was too much for Judy to handle. Her anger surged. Suddenly, Judy grabbed the ladder's bottom rung and yanked back on it. The ladder shook but only moved about six inches.

"What the hell are you doing?" bellowed Jack. "You almost knocked me off this ladder!"

"You've called me a bitch once too often!" screamed Judy. She reached down again, squatting with her knees bent, then lifted as hard as she could muster while stepping backward. The ladder jerked back, shaking Jack at the top. Jack's shifting weight and Judy's pulling action caused the ladder to tumble sideways. Jack screamed as he fell toward the pavement. His paintbrush and can of paint went flying. Jack landed on his back, causing his head to snap violently against the patterned concrete patio with a loud crack. The ladder loudly clanged and rattled as it fell to the pavement while paint splashed in all directions.

Judy stepped back in a foggy daze. She wasn't sure what had just happened. After a few seconds, her mind cleared, and she realized what she had done. Judy moved closer to Jack. A pool of blood was forming from the backside of Jack's head. Blood was also coming out of his nose and mouth. His left arm looked broken, and his right leg was jerking as though it was a spasm. He was alive, but his breathing was shallow.

Judy didn't know what to do. Should she call for help? What if he lived and remembered what had happened? Judy could not stop herself from shaking. Jack soon began to gag on his own blood. Judy's mind raced back and forth from telling herself to help Jack to telling herself to let him die. She knew she should help him, but if Jack lived, he would tell the police what happened, and Judy would go to jail. Judy stared at Jack until his eyes finally rolled back in his head. She heard Jack let out one last moaning sound. He then gasped and stopped breathing.

Judy took a few deep breaths. Realizing Jack was now dead, she became frightened by the potential consequences. She glanced around to see if the adjoining neighbors were outside. Seeing no one, Judy assumed there were no witnesses to what had happened. However, her car was parked out front, so she believed someone had probably seen it. Judy paced in front of Jack's body, contemplating her subsequent actions.

Judy thought it best to call 911 to report that she arrived home and found her husband on the back patio. Before calling, Judy kneeled down beside Jack to check his pulse and breathing. In doing so, she got blood on her hands and clothing. She believed this would make her story more convincing.

After calming herself, Judy dialed 911 on her cell phone.

"911 emergency. How can I help you?"

"I need an ambulance!" screamed Judy. "My husband has fallen!"

"Okay, ma'am, I'll get emergency assistance on the way. What is your name?"

"Judy Kinderman."

"Judy, where has your husband fallen?"

"He fell off a ladder on the back patio." Judy tried to sound panicked.

"Is he still breathing?"

"No! There is blood all over."

"Do you know how to feel for a pulse?"

"Yes."

"Check his pulse for me, please."

Judy kneeled down and reached for Jack's right wrist. She could not find a pulse.

"I can't find a pulse."

"Do you know how to perform CPR?"

"I think so."

"I will talk you through it. Kneel next to your husband and place the palms of your hands on his chest."

"There is blood everywhere!" said Judy. "I hear sirens coming."

"Alright, just stay on the line until medical help arrives. Did you see your husband fall?"

"No. I came home and found Jack lying on the back patio."

The dispatcher kept Judy on the line by asking general questions until help arrived.

"Judy, the EMTs have arrived. They will be with you soon."

"Yes, they are here."

"Okay, Judy. I'm going to hang up now."

The EMTs immediately kneeled next to Jack. One of them used a stethoscope to check his heart. A second EMT set up the automated external defibrillator, commonly known as an AED. They attempted to restart Jack's heart. After several attempts, they stopped their efforts to revive him. The trauma to the back of Jack's head was too severe.

As the EMTs were finishing up, a uniformed Surprise Police Officer walked around the corner of the house. He glanced over the body, then talked briefly with one of the EMTs. He then approached Judy.

"Are you Judy Kinderman?" asked the officer.

"Yes," said Judy, as she sobbed into a handkerchief.

"I'm sorry. Why don't you go inside? I'll join you in a few minutes."

Judy followed the officer's instructions. She got herself a glass of water and looked out the window to the patio. The officer was stringing yellow crime scene tape around the patio. This concerned Judy. *Why is he putting up crime scene tape?*

Judy sat at the dining room table and called Linda Riggs. Linda answered the phone.

"Jack is dead," cried Judy.

"What did you say, Judy?"

"Jack is dead!"

"What? How?"

"I came home to get some things and found him on the back patio. He had fallen off a ladder. He's dead!"

It was challenging to understand Judy through her crying.

"How did he fall?" asked Linda.

"I don't know. I found him on the patio with the ladder lying beside him. He had been painting the house."

"Judy, I'm so sorry. Where are you?"

"In my house. The officer told me to wait inside."

"I'll be over in a few minutes," said Linda.

"Thank you," sobbed Judy.

When she got off the phone, Linda told Ray what had happened.

"You've got to be kidding. Another husband dead?"

"Ray, show some concern. Judy just lost her husband."

Ray was concerned, but he didn't share his thoughts with Linda. Now was not the time.

"How are you always the one to get involved in these ungodly deaths?" asked Ray.

"Just lucky, I guess," said Linda as she grabbed her keys and headed for the door.

It only took Linda eight minutes to arrive at Judy's. Several police cars and a fire truck were parked in the street. She also noticed some neighbors standing outside watching the action.

When Linda entered the house, Judy was seated at the table with a uniformed police officer. The officer was getting basic information from Judy. Linda sat next to Judy and grabbed her hand. Judy squeezed it. Judy told Linda the same story she had given to the officer.

"I'm so sorry, Judy."

"Thank you."

"Can I take Judy away from here now?" asked Linda.

"Not yet," replied the officer. "A detective is on his way to conduct a more thorough interview."

"This was an accident," said Linda.

"Most likely. But we investigate all unattended deaths."

"I see," said Linda. "Thank you."

Linda then peaked between the window blinds onto the patio. "Oh, my god," she blurted, quickly turning away.

Judy looked at Linda. "It's bad, isn't it?"

"I wish I hadn't looked," Linda replied.

After ten minutes, which felt more like thirty to Judy, Detective Dan Baxter arrived. He took a few minutes to observe the accident scene. Judy watched through the window as Baxter bent down to check out Jack's body. She saw Baxter put his hand on Jack's arm. Baxter then touched the spilled paint on the patio concrete and rubbed the wet paint between his thumb and middle finger. He used a wipe to clean his hands. Once he was done, Baxter entered the house and introduced himself to Judy. He then recognized Linda.

"Didn't I just talk to you yesterday at the Hipple residence?" asked Baxter.

Linda nodded her head. "Yes."

"You're a friend of Mary's, correct?"

"Yes, and I'm a friend of Judy's."

"I must say, the odds of you knowing two women whose husbands died within a few days of each other is interesting."

"They are both good friends. That's all there is to it," replied Linda.

"I see." Baxter then turned his attention to Judy.

"Why don't you tell me what happened?" asked Baxter.

Judy explained how she had left her husband and been away from home for a few days. "I returned to the house today for more clothes and personal belongings. Jack's car was here, but I couldn't find him. When I walked out back, I found him lying on the patio. There was blood everywhere."

"Was Jack still alive?" Baxter asked.

"No. I checked on him, but he was already gone."

"Is that how you got blood on your hands and clothing?"

"Yes."

"Did you hear anything as you walked up to the house?"

"No."

"Why did you leave your husband?"

"He was cheating on me. He'd done it multiple times, and I was fed up. I've been staying at a hotel."

"Were you going to divorce him?"

"Yes, that was my intent."

"I assume you know Mary Hipple?"

Judy was surprised by this question. "Uh, yes, I do. What does that have to do with my husband's death?"

"Are you aware Mary's husband was found dead yesterday?"

Judy hesitated before answering. "Yes."

"Why did you hesitate?"

"I was just surprised by the question. What does that have to do with my husband's death?"

"It's just unusual to have two close friends suffer a tragic loss only days apart. And in each case, there were problems in the marriage, and the go-to friend was Linda."

This statement sent a chill down Judy's back. She swallowed. "Well, I'm only concerned about my husband right now."

"I understand. That's all I have for now. We'll take the ladder, paint can, and anything else we can find for evidence. Then I'll do a neighborhood canvass for any witnesses."

This statement made Judy uncomfortable. *I certainly hope there are no witnesses*, thought Judy.

"Why do you need the paint can and ladder?" asked Judy.

"We want to determine the time of the accident and check the ladder for mechanical failure or tampering. I believe you may have just missed seeing your husband fall."

"Why do you say that?"

"Neither the blood nor paint was dry. I'd say Jack fell within minutes of you arriving."

"Damn, maybe if I'd gotten here sooner, this wouldn't have happened," said Judy.

"Maybe. I'll be in touch with our findings," said Baxter.

A female patrol officer entered the house.

"Do you have a change of clothing here?" asked Baxter.

"Yes."

"I need to collect your shoes and clothing. This officer will collect your clothes from you. Once you've done that, you will be free to leave."

"Why do you need my clothing?"

"Just routine. We will examine the paint and blood stains as we would on any unattended death." Baxter then excused himself and went back to the patio.

The female officer followed Judy into the bedroom and collected the clothing as Judy took them off. Each item was packaged in separate paper bags. Once Judy changed, she quickly gathered some of her belongings and left the house.

"Do you need a ride?" asked Linda.

"No, I'm okay to drive. I need to go."

Linda sensed Judy was in a rush. "Drive careful."

Chapter 18

Judy drove a short distance to one of the recreational centers at Cactus View. She sat in her car and called Mary. Mary answered.

"You won't believe this, Mary, but Jack is dead."

"What?! How did Jack die?"

"He fell off a ladder."

"When did this happen?"

"About two hours ago. Can you meet me at my hotel?"

"Okay. Was it the Hampton Inn?"

"Yes, that's the one. I'm on my way there now."

Meanwhile, Linda arrived home and explained to Ray what had happened to Jack.

"How is Judy taking it?" asked Ray.

"She was shaken but seemed to do okay."

"Are you at all suspicious of what has happened in the last two days?" asked Ray.

"I am," admitted Linda. "But until there is proof these deaths are anything other than what they look like, I'm going to support Mary and Judy."

"Just be careful, Linda. The odds of two people we know being found dead in two days are very low."

"I agree," said Linda. "No one else I know better die anytime soon. That detective already thinks it's strange I was at two death scenes in two days."

"Does he think you're involved?"

"I'm not sure," said Linda.

Judy and Mary met in Judy's hotel room. Judy broke down crying as she admitted to Mary what she had done.

Mary put her arm around Judy's shoulders. "It's okay, Judy. If anyone understands your situation, it's me. Your secret is safe with me."

"I know. And your secret is safe with me."

"We can never admit anything to anyone else," said Mary. "No matter what happens, don't tell anyone. Because if you do, the consequences are, well, you know."

"Yes," cried Judy. "I didn't go there to kill Jack. I don't know what happened. I just snapped. He was so infuriating. He didn't even want me to go in the house."

"Men who control their wives are like that, Judy. Women who understand abuse will never fault you."

"I'm not sure the police will see it that way."

"You're right. That's why I'm the only one you can ever tell. When you arrived home, Jack was already dead. As long as you keep your mouth shut, the police won't be able to prove a crime was committed. Do you understand?"

"Yeah, I understand," replied Judy. "But they took my clothing!"

"It's routine to collect all evidence. It doesn't mean they think you committed a crime."

"I guess."

"Have you eaten?" asked Mary.

"No."

"You stay here and rest. I'll get us some food and bring it back here. Do you have any preference?"

"No. Just get whatever you want."

"Alright. I'll be back soon."

Ray Riggs heard a loud knocking at the door. He opened it to find Katy Cullen standing on the porch. She looked upset.

"What's wrong, Katy?"

"Haven't you heard? Jack Kinderman is dead!"

"Yeah, we know."

"Is Linda here? I need to talk to her."

Ray faked a grin. "Sure, come on in."

Linda walked into the living room just as Katy entered the house.

"Jack is dead!" exclaimed Katy.

"Yes, I was there," said Linda.

"YOU were there?"

"Not when it happened. Judy found Jack and called me. I went over to lend my support. It's a terrible accident."

"Accident, my ass!" exclaimed Katy. "Those two have been planning their husband's demise for the last few weeks. And the black widow helped them!"

"Calm down, Katy. You're speculating. You don't know that. Mary was staying with us when Eric committed suicide."

"Do you watch the news? It was reported he had been dead for a couple of days. Mary probably did him in before she left."

"There is plenty of evidence he committed suicide," said Linda.

Katy grunted. "And Judy arrives home just minutes after her husband has an accident?"

Linda didn't respond.

"It's all because of Emily," continued Katy. "She put these ideas into their heads with all her talk of accidents and illnesses."

"Katy, you don't know that. Why don't we allow the police to do their jobs?"

"You know Sharon is quitting the club, right?"

"She hasn't told me that," said Linda.

"Well, she's not happy with all the innuendo about how to murder your spouse."

"What did you tell the police?" asked Linda.

"I've only talked to Detective Begay about Emily. He believes Fred was pushed off the mountain. I told him I agreed. The way Emily talked, she might have killed two husbands."

"You shouldn't have said that. You have no proof."

"She practically admitted it with the way she talks."

Linda ignored the comment. "I will talk to Sharon. As for Mary and Judy, don't jump to conclusions."

"You need to get Emily out of our book club. She's too disruptive."

"You've contributed to that, Katy. You've been judgmental about Emily ever since she joined."

"Who's side are you on?"

"I'm not on any side. Let me ask you this, Katy. Do you like Judy and Mary?"

"Yeah, before all this nonsense."

"Then, at least wait until the police are finished before you accuse them of murder. That's not fair to them."

Katy thought for a minute. "I suppose."

"Now go home, Katy. I'll let you know if I hear anything."

After Katy had left, Ray walked into the room. "I thought you handled that well," he said.

"Thanks. All this drama is wearing me out."

Ray wrapped Linda in his arms. "It will be okay. Like you said, let the police work it all out. I have one question, though."

"Yeah? What is it?"

"Am I on the kill list?"

"Ray!" shouted Linda as she playfully slapped him on the shoulder. "That's not funny!"

As planned, Emily met later that afternoon with Chris Molina in Stonebrook Park. Molina was dressed in a white t-shirt, jeans, and combat boots. His shaved head glistened in the sunlight. They sat at a picnic table while a group of quail picked at the ground nearby.

"What can I do for you?" asked Chris.

"I need you to take someone out and make it look like a robbery."

"Who is this person?"

"The guy I'm living with," said Emily.

"Hmmm. No accident this time?"

"I can't use the same tactics each time. I'm already under suspicion for Fred's death."

"What's his name?"

Emily handed Molina a photograph of Bill. "This is Bill Hutchins. You can have this photo, but destroy it when you're done."

"I know how to do my job, Emily."

"Yeah, I know."

"What has he done to make you want to kill him?"

"Is that important?"

"I have to know why I'm taking someone out. I don't do this for fun, Emily."

"No, of course not. Bill helped me with Fred's accident, and now he's worried because the police have some evidence it wasn't an accident. He's freaking out about it. I'm afraid he's about to crack and admit everything."

"Okay, that's a legitimate reason. When do you want it done?"

"Soon. Make it look like a robbery."

"I need to find him alone somewhere," said Chris.

"Bill plays poker at a club in Surprise every Thursday night. It's called The Eight Ball. It's a pool hall that holds a poker tournament on Thursdays."

"I know the place, but isn't that illegal?" asked Chris.

"Apparently not the way they run it. For a fee, you can play for prizes. You can't win money."

"I see," said Chris.

"At ten o'clock, I will call him and make up a reason to come home. That way, he will leave by himself. You can do it in the parking lot. It's not well lit."

Chris nodded. "Did you bring the money?"

"Yes," said Emily as she reached under the table. She handed Chris a black gym bag. "There's twenty-five thousand, as requested."

"The other half is due the day after it's over," replied Chris.

"Yes, I'm well aware."

"Can I expect a call this Thursday?" asked Chris.

"Yes."

"There's one other thing, Emily."

"What's that?"

"If you get arrested for this, never give the police my name. You know what happens if you do?"

"Yes, I do."

"Okay. You wait here until I'm out of the park, then you can leave."

Emily nodded.

Once Molina was out of sight, Emily left the park and drove home. When she arrived, she could sense Bill was upset.

"Have you heard about Jack?" asked Bill.

"Yes. It's terrible."

"That's two people you and I know in two days! What's going on?"

"Calm down, Bill. I don't know. It's just a coincidence."

"Is this something you're involved in?"

"How could I be involved?" asked Emily.

"Well, you've talked about how rotten their husbands were, and now both are dead."

Emily walked to Bill, then hugged and kissed him. "I can tell you are stressed. Follow me into the bedroom, and I will release your stress."

Bill frowned. "How the hell can you think about sex at a time like this?"

"They're both dead," said Emily. "Nothing we do will change that. Don't be such a coward."

"Coward? I should have never helped you, Emily. This has turned my life upside down. What was I thinking?"

"You're not thinking right now, that's for sure. If you don't pull yourself together, you'll be arrested."

Bill sat at the kitchen table and put his face in his hands, rubbing his forehead with his fingers. "What are we going to do?"

"I promise you, if you stay quiet, you will not be arrested."

"How can you be so sure?" sighed Bill.

"I've taken steps to keep you out of jail."

"What steps?"

"Just trust me. Everything will be okay."

"I sure hope you're right," said Bill.

Emily walked over to Bill and placed her right hand on his shoulder. "I've got everything under control."

Chapter 19

Detective Baxter was eating a sandwich while reviewing reports at his desk when Detective Begay called.

"What's up, Lou?"

"I've heard about your two deaths at Cactus View. What's going on over there?"

"Oh, one was a probable suicide, and in the second one, it appears the victim fell off a ladder while painting his house."

"You're not sure?"

"Eh, there are a few questions," said Baxter. "In the suicide scenario, the victim took a bottle of sleeping pills and lots of alcohol. Blood tests confirmed this. But the guy was naked on top of the bed. Why would he get naked to commit suicide?"

"Good question," agreed Begay.

"We also recovered the whiskey bottle with two sets of fingerprints."

"Anyone live with him?" asked Begay.

"His wife, Mary Hipple."

"Who?"

"Mary Hipple."

There was a pause. "Mary Hipple is a friend of Emily Settlemire. I just recently interviewed her."

"You don't say? That's quite the coincidence."

"How did your accident victim die?" asked Begay.

"He was on an extension ladder and fell while painting his house."

"What's the name?"

"Jack Kinderman."

"Damn. What the hell is going on?"

"What do you mean?"

"Jack's wife is Judy Kinderman, another friend of Emily's. They are all in the same book club!"

"You're telling me that our three cases are linked by friends in a book club?"

"That's what I'm telling you. They all know each other. In my interviews, I've found they've had discussions at their book club meetings on staging accidental deaths."

"They've admitted that?" asked Baxter.

"They said it was concerning the books they've read, but one woman said it was more than that. You need to talk to Katy Cullen. She believes Emily murdered Fred Levine."

"Do you have enough to arrest Emily yet?"

"No. But I should have the DNA results back soon, and Leland is going through the security camera footage from White Tank."

"Something strange is happening in this book club," said Baxter.

"I agree," replied Begay. "A more appropriate name might be the Cactus View Murderer's Club."

After talking with Begay, Baxter called his forensics expert, Scott Taylor. "Scott, how long would it take for fresh paint to dry on painted concrete?"

"That depends on the weather conditions."

"I'm working on a case today that involves a man who fell from a ladder while painting. The paint spilled on the patio. I arrived about half an hour after it was reported, and the paint had thickened but was still sticky to the touch."

"Latex or oil-based?"

"Latex."

"If it was spilled paint, it would be thicker than brushed or rolled paint," said Taylor. "With the temperature today, it should still be sticky or gooey thirty minutes later."

"What about a large pool of blood?"

"About the same, but the blood would dry faster."

"Thanks, Scott."

For Baxter, this confirmed his belief that Jack Kinderman's reported accident occurred close to the time of Judy Kinderman's arrival. Or, maybe even after she had arrived.

The next day, Wednesday, Linda canceled the scheduled book club meeting. Given the circumstances and high emotions, she didn't believe it would be appropriate or productive to have a meeting. Instead, Linda arranged to have Sharon Jansen over for coffee. Sharon arrived as scheduled at ten o'clock.

"Thank you for coming over, Sharon. Would you like cream in your coffee?"

"Yes, please," replied Sharon.

Linda brought out two mugs of coffee and handed one to Sharon. She then tried to convince Sharon not to leave the book club.

"You are a valuable member, Sharon."

"I just can't do it anymore," said Sharon. "I'm too old to be involved in sinister plots. I don't even want to hear talk like that."

As much as she tried, Linda could not change Sharon's mind. "I'm sorry you feel this way, but I understand."

Sharon nodded. "Be careful you don't get caught up in something that gets you in legal trouble."

"I will," promised Linda.

Mary arrived at the Surprise Police Department that afternoon as requested by Detective Baxter. "Thank you for coming, Mary."

"I'm curious why you wanted to talk to me again. I've told you everything I know," said Mary.

"I just have some routine follow-up questions."

"What do you want to know?" asked Mary.

"In processing the scene of your husband's death, I found it strange he was naked. That is unusual. I've never seen that in a suicide. Do you know why he might have been naked?"

"It's common for him to sleep naked," said Mary.

"Does he sleep on top of the blankets?"

"No, not usually."

"When did you last see Eric alive?"

"Like I said before, I left around four o'clock after telling Eric I was going to file for divorce. He became furious. I left before he got physical with me."

"Did he threaten to kill himself?"

"I didn't think so at the time, but I remember Eric saying if I left, I would never see him again."

"You think that was a threat to commit suicide?"

"Not then. But now I do."

"Were you drinking with Eric before you left?"

"No."

"You had nothing to drink?"

"No. I wasn't about to drink before telling Eric I wanted a divorce."

"Is there a reason your fingerprints would be on the whiskey bottle?"

Mary quickly ran the scenario through her head. Did I forget to wipe the prints off the bottle? Mary remembered putting only Eric's prints on the pill bottle and but forgot to wipe the whiskey bottle.

"Mary, did you hear my question?"

"Yes, I'm just trying to remember. The whiskey bottle was in the kitchen. Yes, Eric asked me to bring him the bottle when he was in the living room."

"You carried the bottle to him?"

"Yes."

"When did Eric go into the bedroom?"

"I don't know. When I left, he was still drinking in the living room."

"Where were the sleeping pills when you left?"

"I don't know. Probably in the medicine cabinet."

"Had Eric ever threatened to kill himself?"

"No. He usually threatened me."

"Eric threatened you?"

"Multiple times. He said if I ever left him, he would leave me poor and homeless."

"Were you afraid to leave?"

"Yes. But I couldn't take the abuse anymore," explained Mary.

"Eric abused you?"

"Yes. Both physically and mentally. Even now, I must hire an attorney to help me get my share of the estate. He wouldn't even put the house in my name."

"Sounds like a good reason to kill Eric."

"Excuse me?" said Mary as she sat back in her chair.

"You must admit, Mary, you had the motive and opportunity," said Baxter.

"I didn't kill my husband. He killed himself."

"Who crushed the sleeping pills?"

Mary thought, how does he know about the crushed pills? "I don't know what you're talking about."

"We found residue of the sleeping pills in Eric's glass. Someone dissolved the pills in his drink."

Mary squirmed in her seat, and her mouth felt dry. "It must have been Eric."

"It makes little sense to crush the pills unless you are trying to hide something. Why not just swallow them?"

Mary tried to come up with an answer.

"Mary, did you hear the question?"

"Yes. I don't know, detective."

"I think you do, Mary. The only way out for you was to stage a suicide. Your prints were on that bottle because you were there. Maybe you were drinking with him. After getting Eric drunk, you took sleeping pill powder and mixed it in his drink. Once he was dead, you cleaned up the crime scene. Printing up a suicide note was smart. Avoiding getting your prints on the paper was even smarter. But you forgot about the bottle, didn't you?"

Mary was stunned. She was trying not to shake. "No, I did not kill my husband."

"Well, you had it all worked out beforehand, right?"

"What are you talking about?"

"Didn't Emily tell you how to stage a murder to look like an accident or illness?"

"Huh? No."

"I know Emily talked about it at your book club. I also know you've met with Emily and Judy. Was that when your plan came together?"

"Our book club reads murder mysteries. Katy's probably the one who told you this. Our discussions were always about books we'd read."

"You want me to believe that?"

Mary began to cry. "I don't care what you believe. I'm telling the truth. Are you going to arrest me?"

Baxter hesitated in answering. "Not today. We'll talk again once I have enough for an arrest warrant."

This sent chills down Mary's back. "It's obvious you think I killed Eric. But he committed suicide. I think I need an attorney."

Baxter just sat and looked at Mary. It made Mary nervous as she wondered what Baxter was thinking.

"Unless you're going to arrest me, I'm leaving."

"Okay, Mary, I'll walk you out. Thank you for coming in today."

Mary rushed to her car and immediately phoned Judy.

"Hello."

"Judy, it's Mary. I need to talk to you right now. Where are you?"

Judy could hear the stress in Mary's voice. "Meet me at Cooper's Hawk. We can drink some wine."

"No. It has to be somewhere private."

"Okay. Why don't you meet me at the hotel?"

"Good. I'll be there in about ten minutes."

Judy waited in her room until there was a knock on the door. She opened it, and Mary rushed in.

"He knows!" exclaimed Mary.

"Who knows what?"

"Detective, what's his name, uh, Baxter. He knows I killed Eric!"

"Calm down, Mary. How does he know that?"

"I forgot to wipe my prints from the whiskey bottle. And he knows there were crushed sleeping pills in Eric's drink."

"So what?"

"He said that shows someone, me, wanted to hide the pills in the drink."

"What did you tell him?"

"I said Eric wanted the whiskey bottle, so I handed it to him. And I faked ignorance about the pills."

"But he didn't arrest you."

"No. Not yet. And that bitch, Katy, told him about our book club conversations. I think she also told him about our meeting with Emily. I don't know what Emily will tell him."

"If Emily says anything, she will implicate herself in everything. You don't need to worry about her."

"I guess if I go to prison, I don't need to worry about having money or where to live."

"We may both be there together. I'm meeting with Detective Baxter tomorrow."

"He doesn't believe Jack's death was an accident?"

"The detective wouldn't say. All he told me was he had some questions to clear up."

"Maybe you should get an attorney," said Mary.

"No, I'll be careful what I say. If I get an attorney, it will just make me look guilty."

"I wish Emily would have said something about the sleeping pill residue. I would have at least been prepared," said Mary.

"She probably didn't think of it."

"I thought it was so well planned. I guess those crime shows are right when they say there is no perfect crime."

"In my case, I didn't plan at all. I just reacted," said Judy. "I didn't go home to kill Jack. I may have left all kinds of evidence. He just made me so mad, and I saw an opportunity. My anger took over. I've never responded like that before. I'm not a violent person. But to be honest, I was feeling some envy that you had gotten out of your marriage. Maybe that played some role in how I reacted. I just snapped."

"I understand," said Mary. "But how could they see it as anything but an accident?"

"I'll find out tomorrow, I guess. For now, we're going to calm down and think rationally. From what you've told me, the police don't have a case. Now, I'm going to open this bottle of cabernet so that we can have some wine."

"That sounds great right now," responded Mary.

"Why don't you call Linda to let her know you'll stay with me tonight?"

"I will. Thank you, Judy."

Judy poured two glasses of wine and then swirled the wine in each glass. She handed one glass to Mary, then held up her glass for a toast. Mary did the same.

"To freedom from bad husbands!" said Judy.

"And freedom from jail," said Mary.

Chapter 20

The next day, Judy arrived at the Surprise Police Department at ten o'clock for her interview with Detective Dan Baxter. A clerk at the front desk led Judy to one of the stark interview rooms. She was told to sit on the far side of a small rectangular table. "Detective Baxter will be with you soon."

Judy looked around the small room. The walls were painted a dull gray. In the opposite corner of the ceiling was a camera pointed at Judy. The room felt cool. Suddenly, the door flew open.

"Good morning," said Detective Baxter as he burst through the door. "Thank you for coming in today."

Judy nodded.

"I have some follow-up questions about your husband's death."

"Okay," replied Judy.

"Tell me again how you discovered your husband."

"As I said before, I arrived to pick up more clothing and other things I needed. I saw Jack's car in the open garage. I had hoped he wouldn't be home. When I went inside, I couldn't find Jack, which seemed strange. I then walked outside to the back patio. That's when I saw Jack lying on the patio. Paint was spilled all over, and he looked hurt. I rushed over to him and saw blood around his head and face. I immediately called 911."

"You didn't check to see if he was alive?"

"I could tell he wasn't breathing, so I called 911. The dispatcher then had me check for a pulse. That's when I got blood on myself."

"Was the blood still wet?"

"Yes. Jack must have fallen just before I arrived," cried Judy in her best fake cry.

"We've examined the pants you had on. There are paint spatters on the legs of your pants."

"I suppose there would be," said Judy. "I was stepping in it as I ran to Jack."

Baxter frowned. "The spatters are tiny. That indicates a higher level of impact than just walking around."

"I'm not sure what you are saying," said Judy.

"Well, someone might think you were standing there when the paint fell to the patio. From a height of twelve feet or so, that would create some spatter."

Judy remained calm. "I'm not sure what you're talking about, Detective, but I wasn't there when Jack fell."

"We also found some scrapes on the patio that may have come from the legs of the ladder."

"Okay," said Judy.

"It's almost as though someone had pulled the ladder back."

"Maybe Jack did as he was moving the ladder. I wasn't there, so I can't answer these questions."

Baxter leaned in. "Then why are your fingerprints on the second rung of the ladder?"

This question made Judy shudder. She had to think quickly for an answer. She hesitated.

"Let me think," said Judy. After a pause, she said, "Alright, now I remember. The ladder was across Jack's legs. I grabbed it and moved it off of him."

"You just made that up."

"I did not make it up. My mind was swirling that day. The fact that I didn't remember a tiny detail is understandable, don't you think?"

Baxter wasn't giving up. "Possibly. Or maybe you are covering up the fact that you had planned to kill your husband."

"My god, what are you talking about?"

"I know about your discussions with Emily."

Judy faked ignorance. "Huh?"

"The discussions at your book club meetings and the meetings you've had with Mary and Emily where you discussed how to stage accidents or illnesses."

Judy had expected this to come up, so she was prepared. Judy laughed. "You must be talking about crazy Katy. She has one hell of an imagination. Maybe you should arrest all the members of the club. We talk about how murders are committed all the time as part of our book discussions."

"You had motive, Judy. With all of Jack's cheating, I wouldn't blame you for wanting him dead."

"I wanted out of the marriage. I didn't want Jack dead. If you can't distinguish an accident from a murder, you're not much of a detective."

"Well, I know you, Mary, and Linda are good friends. I also know you talk regularly to Emily, who seems to be the ringleader."

"You are right, Detective. We are friends. It doesn't make me a murderer."

Baxter smiled. "Alright, Judy. That's all for today."

"I'm free to go?"

"Yes."

Judy walked out of the police department feeling proud of herself. Rarely was she so assertive, but Judy knew she had to perform well or risk being arrested. Knowing how Mary had been interrogated helped prepare Judy for the worst. The evidence cited by Detective Baxter worried her, but Judy believed he would have arrested her if it were enough to charge her.

On her way back to the hotel, Judy called Mary.

"How'd it go?" asked Mary.

"Hard to tell, but I think I did okay. Talking to you beforehand helped me prepare for some of the questions."

"Is he going to close the case?" asked Mary.

"I'm not sure. The wet blood and paint were an issue. They also found my fingerprints on the ladder."

"Oh, I hadn't thought of that," said Mary.

"Neither had I. I had to think quickly. I told the detective I had to move the ladder."

"Did he believe you?"

"I'm not sure. He brought up our meeting with Emily."

"If Emily ever tells the truth, we are in trouble, Judy."

"She won't. Emily has too many skeletons in her own closet. I'm not worried about her."

"Everyone has a breaking point," said Mary. "As we see on Forty-eight Hours and other crime shows, suspects often make deals to improve their own situation."

"Let's not worry about that now," said Judy. "How about us going out for dinner tonight? We need some fun time."

"That sounds fantastic. Six o'clock?"

"Sure. How does Sakura sound? I'm in the mood for some Japanese grilling."

"Great, I'll see you back at the hotel," said Mary.

Late that afternoon, Detective Baxter was at his desk reviewing his interview notes when his phone rang. He could see it was Detective Begay calling.

"What's up, Lou?"

"We finally got some results back on the DNA. The DNA mixture on Levine's shirt contained the DNA of Bill Hutchins."

"Hot damn!" exclaimed Baxter. "I knew Levine had to have been pushed."

"Oh, there's one more thing," said Begay.

"Yeah?"

"After going through hundreds of security photos, Ashford found a photo of Emily and Fred entering the park."

"What about Hutchins?"

"He wasn't in the car."

"Well, that doesn't help."

"No, but Ashford kept looking. Ten minutes later, he sees a silver Toyota Camry entering the park."

"That's what Hutchins drove," said Baxter.

"Yes. Behind the wheel, you can clearly see Bill Hutchins. He was definitely there that day."

"Lou, you just made your case."

"Yep. I'll be working on arrest warrants for both Emily and Bill over the weekend. With the complexity of this case, I need to get it right."

"I agree. Given that my victims were associated with Emily and that damn book club, I'd like to be there when you do the interrogations. Maybe we can squeeze her for information on Mary Hipple and Judy Kinderman."

"Yeah, no problem. You can even help me with the arrests."

"I'd like that. Congratulations, Lou."

At 5:05 p.m., Chris Molina scoped out the surroundings in the Eight Ball pool hall parking lot. He was pleased to find the business faced a side street. His only concern was the small independent liquor store across the street from the pool hall. Molina plotted out his escape route. If Hutchins parked on the south side, Molina would park a block south. If Hutchins parked on the north side, Molina would park a block north. He hoped Hutchins would park on the south side, as that provided a less busy escape route. Molina then looked for security cameras. He found one near the front entrance. Based on where it was directed, he believed he could avoid coming into view of the camera. The big unknown and greatest danger was whether anyone else would be in the parking lot at ten o'clock. Molina planned to wear a dark, hooded sweatshirt. Even so, should a bystander get a good look at him, he had to be prepared to take out the witness.

It was 6:15 p.m. when Emily arrived home carrying a take-out order from Dicky's Barbecue.

"What's this?" asked Bill.

"Dinner. You've had a tough week, and I thought I'd get you one of your favorites."

Bill could smell the smokey barbecue meat. "It smells delicious. What did you get?"

"Pulled pork and chicken with mashed potatoes, green beans, and cornbread. I also have a bottle of wine."

"What's the celebration?"

"Nothing. I just told you it was because of your tough week."

"Well, thank you, Emily."

"You're welcome. I wanted you to have a wonderful dinner before your poker challenge tonight."

"Thanks, but I don't think I'll go tonight."

Emily paused. "You have to go."

"Why do I have to go?"

"Bill, it's important to keep up your routine. If you change now, it may look more suspicious to the police. They will think you are hiding from the public eye."

"I don't know, Emily. I'm so nervous about all this."

"Which is why you have to go. Get your mind off the investigation. I went to the trouble of getting you one of your favorite dinners. I insist you go. I have some friends coming over tonight, and I don't want you getting in my way."

"Oh, all right. I'll go."

"It will be fun, Bill. Now come over here, sit down, and enjoy this dinner I took all day preparing."

Bill chuckled.

"See? You're already feeling better."

After eating and two glasses of wine, it was time for Bill to leave. "When are your friends coming over?"

"I told them eight o'clock. I knew you would be gone by then. Doesn't your poker game start at eight?"

"Yes. I should get moving." Bill grabbed his wallet and car keys. "The game lasts until eleven. I should be home by eleven-thirty."

"Have fun, Bill."

Bill smiled as he walked out the door.

Chris Molina was home preparing his black Glock model 22 semi-automatic handgun. The Glock 22 was a popular model, shooting forty caliber bullets from a magazine. It was a popular gun among police officers. Molina liked it because it was smaller and held more bullets than most. With hollow point bullets, the Glock 22 was deadly efficient. Finally, Molina liked that the safety was built into the trigger. There was never a need to release a safety before firing.

The plan was for Molina to call Emily on his burner phone once he was in place and the parking lot was clear of witnesses. Emily would then call Bill with an excuse for him to come home. As Bill approached his car, Molina would confront him, shoot him in the chest, then take his wallet to make it look like a robbery.

At 9:30 p.m., Molina drove to the club in his old brown Ford Bronco. He slowly drove past to scout the area. Nothing seemed out of the ordinary. There were multiple cars parked in the dimly lit parking lot. Bill's new black BMW, a present from Emily, was parked nose-in against the building on the south side. Molina drove past the lot to the side street on the south side of the club and parked along the street. Molina exited the car dressed in a black hooded sweatshirt and blue jeans. Once out of the car, he pulled the hood over his head. Molina then walked toward the parking lot, scanning the area with his eyes. The parking lot was empty of people and dimly lit.

Molina found a large pickup truck to squat behind. At approximately 9:50 p.m., Molina used his burner phone to call Emily. Once Emily answered, Molina's only words to her were "go time." He then disconnected.

Emily took a deep breath to calm her nerves. She then dialed Bill on her cell phone. He answered.

"What is it?" asked Bill.

"I accidentally cut myself, and I need you to take me to the hospital."

"What happened?"

"I was cutting some fruit and sliced my hand. There is blood everywhere."

"Do you want me to call an ambulance?"

"No, no. I have pressure on the cut, but I need stitches. Can you come home, please?"

"Yes, of course. Let me pull out of this game, and I will be there soon."

"Thank you, Bill."

Bill briefly explained the situation at home and excused himself from the poker game. Bill then left, walking briskly to the parking lot.

From behind the truck, Molina saw a man walking from the club door toward the black BMW. As the man approached, Molina could tell it was Bill Hutchins. Molina waited until Bill was at the driver's side door before jumping out from cover. He quickly approached Bill with his gun raised and said, "Hold it!"

Bill was startled as he looked at Molina. "What the hell?"

"Give me your wallet!"

"Huh?"

"I said give me your wallet, or you're a dead man."

"Yeah, yeah. Okay. Don't shoot," said Bill as he reached into his back left pocket and pulled out his wallet. "Here you go."

As soon as Molina grabbed the wallet from Bill's hand, he took a step back, raised the Glock 22 and pointed it at Bill's chest.

"What are you...."

BAM! BAM! BAM!

Molina fired three rapid shots into Bill's chest. Bill immediately collapsed to the ground.

Molina turned and ran as fast as he could across the parking lot to the street on the south side. He jumped into his Ford Bronco, fired it up, and promptly drove away.

Patrons inside the Eight Ball heard the shots. Several men exited the club to see what was happening. None of them could see anything at first. Then, one man pointed out an interior car light was on. Three men walked toward the car with the light. As they came upon the open driver's door, they saw Bill lying on his side in a large pool of blood.

"Call 911!" shouted one of the men.

Another man leaned down and rolled Bill onto his back. The front of Bill's gray polo shirt was soaked in blood. The man checked for a pulse but could not find one. Other club patrons soon gathered outside to observe. Within minutes, sirens filled the air as Surprise police officers arrived on the scene. The first officers to arrive moved everyone back from Bill's car. One of the officers looked at Bill and knew he was dead.

Several minutes later, a medical unit arrived. The EMTs were directed to Bill. A quick medical evaluation confirmed what the officers already knew. Bill Hutchins was dead.

Chapter 21

Chris Molina drove to a vacant church parking lot. After removing $75 in cash from Bill's wallet, Molina walked to a dumpster behind the church and chucked the wallet into the trash. He returned to his car to call Emily.

"Hello," answered Emily.

"It's done," said Molina. "Meet me with the money in the Costco parking lot on Waddell tomorrow at two o'clock."

"Why Costco?

"Because there will be lots of activity there. No one will even notice us. We'll make the exchange in my car. I'll be in my brown Bronco parked on the northeast side."

"Are you sure Bill is dead?"

"I made sure there was no doubt. Three shots right into the heart."

Emily cringed at the words. While she believed it was necessary to eliminate Bill, Emily still hated the thought of Bill being gunned down. She had really liked him.

"Okay, I'll see you tomorrow then," said Emily.

Detective Dan Baxter was home watching the nightly news when his cell phone rang.

"Detective, it's Sergeant Sheila Andrews. Sorry to bother you, but we've just had a homicide at the Eight Ball Club. It appears to be a robbery. One male victim is dead from at least three gunshots to the chest, and his wallet is missing."

"Damn. Was it inside the club?"

"No. The shooting occurred in the parking lot. We have the scene taped off."

"I'm on my way," said Baxter.

It didn't take long for Baxter to grab what he needed and be on his way to the crime scene. While driving, Baxter couldn't help but wonder what was happening in the City of Surprise. He was facing the possibility of having three homicides in one week. There were entire years when Surprise wouldn't have three homicides. At least this one didn't sound related to a book club, he chuckled to himself.

Baxter arrived at a chaotic scene. All the medical personnel had left, but numerous officers were still on the scene, and patrons from the bar were gathered to mourn and watch the police activity. Sergeant Sheila Andrews briefed Detective Baxter on what little they knew. It appeared to be a random robbery at gunpoint. Baxter asked Andrews if the victim had been identified.

"The Arizona plate lists to William Hutchins," said Andrews.

"William Hutchins?" asked Baxter.

"Yes."

"Oh, my god," replied Baxter.

"What is it, Dan?" asked Andrews.

"Bill Hutchins is a suspect in a Maricopa County case from last September. And that case may be related to two more homicides in the Cactus View community."

"If you're right, this may not have been a robbery," said Andrews.

"No, and I already have a suspect in mind," replied Baxter.

Baxter then walked into the crime scene to observe the victim. The victim was lying flat on his back. Baxter bent over the victim, then shined his flashlight on the victim's face. "Yep, that's Bill Hutchins," said Baxter to no one.

Baxter then examined Hutchins' front shirt. Although it was soaked in blood, Baxter could see three holes in the shirt, all in a tight pattern over the heart. He then stood up and turned toward Sergeant Andrews.

"This was not a robbery," said Baxter. "Based on the pattern of shots, our victim was standing and not moving. This indicates the victim was not fighting back or trying to run when shot. Why would a robber shoot a victim who was not resisting?"

"I don't know," said Andrews. "We also have a witness you might want to talk to. Her name is Sunshine Summer. She's standing right over there."

Baxter shined his flashlight at Summer. "What's all that crap on her neck and right cheek?"

"Those would be tattoos, Dan."

"Sunshine Summer with the tattoos. Got it," replied Baxter.

Summer was a twenty-three-year-old white female with long blond hair. She was wearing a tight-knit shirt, and she obviously had no bra. Summer had been in the liquor store across the street purchasing a twelve-pack of Corona beer. When she exited the store, she heard gunshots from the parking lot of the Eight Ball.

Baxter walked over to Summer and introduced himself. "I'm Detective Baxter. I understand you witnessed something?"

"Yeah. I was coming out of the liquor store across the street when I heard loud bangs coming from the parking lot of the Eight Ball. I recognized them as gunshots. I didn't see the shooting, but I saw a man running south and around the corner of the building."

"What did this man look like?" asked Baxter.

"He wasn't big. It was dark, but I believe he was a white male. He was wearing a black sweatshirt with a hoodie."

"Did you see him carrying a gun?"

"No."

"Did you see him get into a car?"

"No. Once he got around the corner, I couldn't see where he went."

"Do you know what time it was?"

"It was just before ten o'clock."

"You said you believed he was white. You're not sure?"

"I could see his face in the dark. He looked white to me."

"Okay, thank you, Sunshine. Does the Sergeant have your contact information?"

"Yes."

"Great. We will call you if we have more questions. Here is my card if you think of anything else."

After Baxter had finished interviewing Sunshine, Sergeant Andrews approached him again.

"Some of the club patrons are telling officers our victim received a phone call from his girlfriend just before he left the club. Apparently, the girlfriend had cut herself and needed to be taken to a hospital."

Baxter wanted to be sure he heard the information correctly. "Witnesses are saying the girlfriend called our victim just before he left to be gunned down?" he asked.

"That's what they're saying," said Andrews.

"I think I know who called him," said Baxter. "His live-in girlfriend is Emily Settlemire. She is already a suspect in a county case."

"Are you referring to the death in White Tank Mountain Park?"

"Yes. Lou Begay started on arrest warrants for Emily and tonight's victim earlier today."

"That's interesting."

"He certainly won't need one for Bill Hutchins now," said Baxter.

After talking with Sergeant Andrews, Baxter called Detective Lou Begay.

Begay answered. "Kind of late to be making a social call."

"Yeah, and you won't believe what I'm about to tell you," said Baxter.

"Okay. Shock me then."

"Bill Hutchins was gunned down in the parking lot of the Eight Ball tonight."

There was a pause on the phone. "Are you serious, Dan?"

"I'm serious. At least you won't need to get an arrest warrant for Hutchins."

"Damn," replied Begay. "Any ideas yet?"

"My guess is the woman who has been driving this from the beginning set this up. Emily Settlemire."

"You think Emily shot Bill?" asked Begay.

"No. This was set up to look like a robbery. Hutchins took three to the chest. You don't see that in a simple robbery. Whoever shot him wanted to be sure Hutchins was dead. Witnesses are telling us Hutchins received a call from his girlfriend just before he left the club. That must be Emily. From across the street, a witness heard gunshots, then saw a white male wearing a dark hooded sweatshirt running from the scene."

"Given what you're telling me, it may have been a contract killing," said Begay.

"That's what I'm thinking," said Baxter. "And Emily Settlemire is my prime suspect. I will work on a warrant for access to her phone records tomorrow."

"I should have a warrant by late tomorrow for her arrest on Fred Levine's death," said Begay. "We can then interrogate her together."

"I will look forward to that," replied Baxter.

By the time Baxter was finished, the coroner had arrived and was loading Bill's body into the coroner's van. Sergeant Andrews approached Baxter and handed him an envelope.

"What is this?" asked Baxter.

"Three shell casings were found near the victim's car. All forty caliber."

"Thank you," said Baxter.

"What's wrong, Dan? You look worried."

"I am worried, Sheila. In five months, we have four men dead from the same circle of friends. Three of them have died this week. At least two of them are the result of homicides, and the other two might be."

"Are these all related to the Cactus View community?"

"Yes, and specifically to a group of women in a book club."

"Well, you know how those retired folks are when they're angry about something," replied Andrews. "They can get upset about everything from politics to the cost of an ice cream cone."

Baxter laughed. "I suppose you're right. But resorting to homicide seems a bit much. Did you recover our victim's cell phone?"

"Yes, I have it bagged and in my car."

"Thank you, Sheila. Unless you need something else from me, I'm going to the office to start on my paperwork."

"I think we have it covered. I'll call you if we find any other surprises," said Andrews.

When he returned to the police department, Baxter immediately began working on an affidavit for a search warrant on Emily Settlemire's cell phone. He wanted to complete most of it before Detective Begay obtained an arrest warrant for Emily. Once an arrest warrant was approved, it would be easy to get the warrant for Emily's phone records. Baxter also believed it would be more effective to confront Emily after her arrest for Fred Levine's murder.

By the time Baxter completed his affidavit for the phone records, it was after midnight. He then drove to his home in the Marley Park neighborhood. His wife, Lisa, was waiting for him.

"How bad was it?" asked Lisa.

"The victim didn't suffer. He was hit with three to the chest in a tight pattern from close range. We believe it was an arranged killing. And get this, it was the guy the county believes pushed Fred Levine off the mountain."

"Do you think they're related?" asked Lisa.

"Definitely. The four deaths we've had from last September to this week are connected to that book club I've told you about. And specifically, to a woman named Emily Settlemire."

"Are you going to arrest her?"

"The county should have a warrant for her arrest sometime tomorrow. I'm working with Lou Begay on the case, and I look forward to interrogating that woman again."

"Are you coming to bed soon?"

"In a little while. I'm not sure I could sleep right now."

Baxter grabbed a beer from the refrigerator, sat on the leather living room couch, reclined the seat, and turned on the TV. He then flipped through the channels until he found old re-runs of Seinfeld. He figured a couple episodes of Seinfeld would clear his mind and help him sleep. Unfortunately, even after two beers and several episodes of Seinfeld, Baxter had difficulty sleeping. All he could think about was that crazy book club and all the associations with dead men. He knew the next day would be a busy one.

Chapter 22

After about five hours of restless sleep, Baxter showered, ate a light breakfast of toast and coffee, then headed to work. He arrived at seven forty-five. His first task was to call Maricopa County Detective Lou Begay.

"Are you at work yet?" asked Baxter.

"No. I work for the county. We usually stroll in between nine-thirty and ten o'clock," joked Begay.

"I know you guys are lazy, but we have dead bodies piling up over here," replied Baxter.

"What do you want?" asked Begay in a sarcastic tone.

"I have an idea. What if we put a tail on Settlemire? With everything that's happened in the last week, we should keep tabs on what she's doing. If she hired someone to kill Hutchins, I'm guessing she will have to meet the killer somewhere to exchange the payoff."

"That's actually a good idea," said Begay. "You city cops are sometimes smarter than you look."

"I'm drinking coffee to stay awake, and you're cracking jokes. How many more cases does a city cop need to solve for you?"

Begay laughed. "I can ask Leland if he's available to help. Do you have anyone over there?"

"Yes. Denise Gibbs is one of our new detectives. She's willing to help," said Baxter.

"Hang on a second," said Begay.

Baxter waited for Begay to come back on the phone. After about twenty seconds, Begay came back on.

"Yes, Leland can help. I'll send him over to your office. I need to stay here and work on this warrant."

"I understand," said Baxter. "I'll coordinate the surveillance with Leland and Denise."

Thirty minutes later, Detective Leland Ashford met with Baxter at the police department.

"I've already sent Detective Gibbs out to sit on Emily's house," said Baxter. "She'll let us know if Emily leaves the house."

"What do you need from me?" asked Ashford.

"You and I simply need to set up near Cactus View and wait for Emily to leave. The three of us will then coordinate following her."

"Where would you like me to go?"

"Why don't you set up at the nearby Fry's supermarket? I will set up somewhere off Waddell Road."

"Sounds good," said Ashford.

Both detectives left and drove to their assigned area to wait. They knew it could be a long day. Gibbs had parked a block away from Hutchins' home, the house Emily lived in.

Now that Bill was dead, Emily was the only occupant. Gibbs could see the garage and driveway from where she parked.

Meanwhile, Detective Begay worked on getting a warrant for Emily's arrest for the murder of Fred Levine. He knew it would be more challenging to establish probable cause of Emily's involvement with Hutchins now dead. With the DNA development and video of Hutchins following Fred and Emily into the park, his plan had been to arrest Hutchins first. Begay believed Hutchins would crack under the pressure and admit it was Emily behind the planning for Fred's murder. With Hutchins' death, he now had to craft his affidavit to convince a judge that Emily was in cahoots with Bill. His affidavit would include Katy Cullen's statements about comments made by Emily. It wasn't the most robust evidence, but Begay hoped a judge would agree there was probable cause to arrest Emily Settlemire.

It was almost noon, and no one had left or arrived at Emily's home. Baxter called Gibbs to find out if she needed a break.

"Yes, I could use a bathroom and grab some lunch," Gibbs said.

"I'm almost there," said Baxter. "Once I pull up behind you, take your break."

"Thanks, Dan."

Baxter then called Ashford. "I'm relieving Denise while she takes a break. Would you like me to take your place after I leave here?"

"Not necessary," said Ashford. "I've got everything I need here at Fry's."

Meanwhile, word of Bill Hutchins' death spread quickly throughout the Cactus View community. News of the shooting had been on all the morning news programs.

Linda Riggs had received multiple calls throughout the morning. The most animated one was from Katy Cullens.

"Did you hear the news about Bill?" shouted Katy.

"You don't have to yell, Katy. I can hear you just fine. Yes, I heard about Bill. It's a terrible tragedy."

"I warned you about Black Widow Emily, but you wouldn't listen. She has her hand in these killings!"

"Katy, can we at least wait until the investigations are completed? The news is saying Bill was robbed last night by a hooded white male."

"I'm telling you, Linda. Emily had him killed. I never liked that woman. What did you ever see in her?"

"Katy, I won't allow you to blame me for anything. None of us are to blame, even if what you say is true."

"Are you going to at least boot her out of book club?"

"I've already told her not to attend meetings until this mess is cleared up. Now I've got to go." Linda hung up the phone without saying goodbye.

"That must have been Katy," said Ray.

"Yes, it was," grumbled Linda. "She may be right about Emily, but her attitude is irritating."

"She's always been irritating," said Ray.

"Yes, but not to this extent. I do hope Katy is wrong about Mary and Judy. They are both wonderful friends. It would crush me if they were to be arrested."

"You know Mary is innocent. She was with us the night Eric committed suicide," said Ray.

"I've read all the news reports, and while I think it is unlikely, Eric could have been dead before Mary came over that night," said Linda.

"You could hardly blame her for killing him after all the abuse she took. But you're right; I'd hate to see her go to prison."

"I tried calling both Mary and Judy, but neither answered," said Linda. "I'm worried about them. Normally, they would have called me about something like this."

When they heard about Bill's death, Mary Hipple and Judy Kinderman had just finished breakfast. They were saddened by the news of his death but also worried it would bring further suspicion onto them. When Linda attempted to call them, neither answered their phone.

"Do you think Emily is behind this?" asked Judy.

"The news is reporting he was killed in a robbery by a white male," answered Mary.

"Yeah, but what are the odds Emily would lose her boyfriend soon after losing her husband?"

"She's lost two husbands," Mary reminded her.

"Yes, and now the man she was living with. The police must see it as more than a coincidence."

"Yeah, I'm worried too," agreed Mary. "Our association with Emily will put more scrutiny on the deaths of our husbands."

"Maybe we should leave town," suggested Judy.

"No. That would place more suspicion on us. We need to continue on as though our husbands died precisely as we told it."

Detective Gibbs returned to her surveillance post at 12:50 p.m. "Thank you for the break, Dan."

"My pleasure," said Baxter. "I'm going to get myself a sandwich and then find a place to park. Let us know if you see anything."

After stopping at Whataburger to pick up a burger and soda, Baxter set up in a parking lot off Waddell near Highway three-o-three. The time was 1:10 p.m. Baxter called Begay to check on the status of his arrest warrant.

"I'm almost finished with the affidavit. I've also included a request for Emily's phone records on this case," said Begay. "There may have been some back and forth between Emily and Bill on the day of Fred's murder."

"Terrific," said Baxter. "When will you present it to a judge?"

"I have an appointment with Judge Little at two o'clock."

"Great. I'll let you know if anything happens out here. Thus far, Emily hasn't left the house."

"Okay," said Begay. "Keep me posted."

Baxter made himself as comfortable as possible, turned his radio to a country station, and bit into his juicy burger. As he finished his meal, Baxter received a text from the medical examiner's office. According to the message, three forty-caliber hollow point bullets were recovered from Bill Hutchins' body. One bullet was intact enough for comparison against the murder weapon when or if it was found. *This is good news*, thought Baxter.

At 1:50 p.m., Baxter's police radio squawked. "Suspect is leaving her residence now. Driving a red Lexus with an Arizona plate."

Baxter sat up, waiting to hear what direction Emily would go. Ashford maneuvered his car in the Fry's parking lot to allow a quick exit.

"Looks like she is turning right onto Greenway," said Gibbs. "Coming your way, Leland."

Ashford was ready to pull in behind Emily should she pass Fry's Market.

"We're at Cotton Lane now," said Gibbs. "She's going to turn south on Cotton Lane."

Ashford could see the red Lexus pass by as it continued south on Cotton Lane. Ashford pulled out behind Emily as Gibbs backed off. He continued to follow Emily to Waddell Road.

"She's in the left turn lane at Waddell," said Ashford.

"I'm just east of you on Waddell," said Baxter. "I'll take over as she passes by."

"Okay, she turned left. Heading east on Waddell," said Ashford.

Baxter was on Waddell just east of Costco.

"It looks like she's going to turn into the Costco parking lot," said Ashford.

"Great," said Baxter. "We waited this long to watch her go shopping. I see her pulling in now. Once she parks, I'll set up east of her while you set up west."

"Got it," replied Ashford.

"Denise, you hang back as the chase car once she leaves."

"Copy," said Gibbs.

Baxter watched as Emily slowly drove down an entire parking lane. She passed multiple open spots. Emily then made a U-turn and started slowly down a second lane.

"She's just trolling the parking lot right now," said Baxter. "Hold on. Looks like she's finally parking. I've got eyes on her."

About a minute passed.

"She's now getting out of the car carrying a brown briefcase. Maybe this is the payoff. Standby."

"Okay," said Baxter. "She's on foot approaching a brown Ford Bronco. Can you see it, Leland?"

"Yeah, I see it. Someone's sitting in the driver's seat. Looks like a white male."

"Alright, she's now getting in the passenger side," said Baxter.

"It looks like they're having a conversation," said Ashford.

"We're not going to let them leave," said Baxter. "If he starts the car, I'm pulling up to block him."

"I'll come from the other way," said Ashford.

"I have the west side covered if they run," said Gibbs.

"This has to be the payoff," said Baxter. "Screw it. I'm not taking any chances. I'm pulling behind them now."

Baxter pulled up in his detective car and stopped directly behind the brown Bronco, preventing the driver from backing out. He saw Ashford coming down the lane from the opposite direction. Gibbs quickly moved her car in position west of the suspect vehicle, one lane over. Baxter promptly exited his car with his handgun drawn. He rushed to the driver's door, shouting, "Police! Get your hands up! Get your hands up!"

Chris Molina was startled and reached for his handgun. However, he quickly realized it was the police. He removed his hand from his gun and raised both hands. Emily was shocked and confused by the screaming. As Baxter and Ashford approached Molina, Emily exited the passenger door.

"Freeze!" shouted Detective Gibbs, while pointing her handgun at Emily.

"What?" yelled Emily. "I haven't done anything!"

"Hands in the air," ordered Gibbs.

Emily did as she was told. As Baxter and Ashford pulled Molina out of the car, Gibbs placed Emily in handcuffs behind her back.

Baxter and Ashford shoved Molina against the side of the Bronco. Baxter searched Molina and recovered a forty-caliber Glock handgun from the holster on his belt. He then placed Molina in handcuffs.

"Is this what you used to gun down Bill Hutchins?" shouted Baxter as he waved the gun.

"I don't know what you're talking about," replied Molina.

"Sure you don't."

"Why are you arresting me?" cried Emily.

Gibbs ignored her question.

"Leland, see what's in that briefcase," ordered Baxter.

Ashford reached into the Ford Bronco and pulled out a brown briefcase. He snapped open the latches and opened the top. Stacks of hundred-dollar bills were neatly arranged in the case.

Baxter looked at Emily. "Is that what Bill Hutchins' life was worth?"

"I don't know what you're talking about," replied Emily.

Baxter looked at Gibbs. "Take the bitch to the police holding room."

"Got it," replied Gibbs.

"You're arresting me!" shouted Emily. "He was blackmailing me! What have I done?"

"Let's go," said Gibbs as she walked Emily toward her car.

"Leland, if you stay here and get this car impounded, I'll take this asshole to the police station," said Baxter.

"No problem, Dan."

On the way to the police station, Molina wanted to know what he was being arrested for.

"Are you serious?" asked Baxter. "You're under arrest for the homicide of Bill Hutchins."

"I haven't killed anybody."

"Yeah? Well, I'll bet that gun we took off of you will match the bullets we took out of Bill Hutchins' chest."

After that comment, Molina remained quiet for the rest of the ride.

Gibbs wasn't so lucky. For the entire ride to the police station, Emily Settlemire loudly proclaimed her innocence. She claimed to have met Chris Molina at Costco only to hire him to find the person who robbed and murdered Bill.

"I'm sure Detective Baxter will ask you all about it," said Gibbs.

Once they had arrived at the police department, Baxter placed Molina in a secure interview room. He told Gibbs to lock Emily in a holding cell. Baxter wanted to give Begay time to arrive for Emily's interview.

After locking Emily in the holding cell, Emily screamed at Gibbs. "Why are you locking me up? I haven't done anything!"

"Calm down, Emily," said Gibbs. "You'll get your chance to explain everything. Would you like something to drink?"

"Yes. Get me a margarita."

Gibbs frowned. "I'll get you some water."

Baxter allowed Molina to wait in the interview room until Ashford had returned. They then entered the interview room together.

"Chris, I'm Detective Dan Baxter with the Surprise Police Department, and this is Detective Leland Ashford with the Sheriff's Department. We want to ask you some questions, but first, I need to read your Miranda Rights. After Baxter finished, he asked Chris if he would answer some questions.

"Depends on what you want to ask," replied Chris.

"I'll start with an easy one," said Baxter. "Where do you live?"

"I have an apartment in El Mirage."

"And how do you know Emily Settlemire?"

"She's a nurse I met at urgent care. I used to have a drug problem."

"Do you still have a drug problem?"

"I've been clean for fourteen months."

"Well, congratulations. Tell us why you were meeting with Emily today."

"She wanted to hire me to find out who killed her boyfriend."

"Emily wanted to hire you as a private investigator?"

"I guess so."

"Are you a private investigator?"

"I know lots of people in the area. I'm good at getting information."

"Detective Gibbs told me there was twenty-five thousand dollars in that briefcase. Was she going to pay you that much up front?"

"I guess."

"Were you at the Eight Ball Club last night?"

"No."

"Are you sure? Someone saw you there."

Chris was taken aback by this statement. "I wasn't there."

"You know Bill Hutchins was shot there last night, right?"

"Yes. That's what Emily wanted me to investigate."

"Chris, before you get too wrapped up in lies, let me explain something to you," said Baxter. "We have a witness who saw you in a dark hooded sweatshirt running from the scene immediately after the shooting. We took a forty-caliber Glock handgun from you today, and we have the bullets removed from Hutchins' chest. I'm betting those bullets will match your gun. Strike number three is we caught you today amid a large payout from Emily. Strike four will be when Emily tries to protect herself by saying you were blackmailing her for information about Bill's shooting."

Chris stared at the table.

"What do you have to say, Chris?"

"I want a lawyer."

"Okay, we're done here then," said Baxter.

Baxter and Ashford both got up to leave.

"Am I free to leave?" asked Chris.

Baxter chuckled. "No, Chris. You're going to be booked on a murder charge. And after we get Emily's statement, probably a conspiracy charge as well."

They left Chris locked in the room. Baxter then asked Gibbs to book Chris on a murder charge.

"Did he confess?" asked Gibbs.

"No. We need either the bullet to match or Emily's confession for a solid case," said Baxter.

Ashford called Begay to tell him about Emily's arrest and to find out when his arrest warrant for Levine's murder would be completed.

"I'm in the judge's chamber now. If all goes well, I'll have an arrest warrant soon."

"Good. We are waiting for you to arrive before interviewing Emily."

"I appreciate that," said Begay. "I'll get there as soon as I can."

After twenty minutes, the judge finished reading the affidavit and signed an arrest warrant on Emily for the murder of Fred Levine. Begay called Baxter.

"I've got the arrest warrant. I'm on my way."

"Fantastic. We'll be waiting for you in the interrogation room."

Chapter 23

Judy and Mary were having an early dinner when Judy's phone rang. It was Linda calling again.

"I better answer this," said Judy. "This is the fourth time Linda has called."

"Hello."

"Judy, where have you been?" asked Linda. "I've been worried about you. I thought you might have been arrested."

"Arrested? No. I'm having an early dinner with Mary right now."

"Sorry to interrupt, but do you know about Bill?"

"Yes. Terrible news."

"I think Emily has been arrested," said Linda.

"Emily's been arrested? For what?"

"I think it's for Bill's murder. A neighbor of mine was at Costco earlier, and there was a commotion in the parking lot. The police were arresting two people. My neighbor recognized one of them as Emily."

"Oh, my god," said Judy.

"What is it?" asked Mary.

Judy didn't respond to Mary's question.

"I wanted to be sure you and Mary were okay," said Linda.

"Why would you think we weren't?"

"Well, I know the police have some suspicions. I was afraid maybe you and Mary had been arrested."

"No, we're both fine."

"Alright, I'll let you get back to your dinner. Sorry to bother you."

"No bother, Linda. Thank you for telling us about Emily."

After Judy got off her phone, Mary asked what the problem was.

"Emily has been arrested."

"Arrested? For what?" asked Mary.

"Linda thinks it might be for Bill's murder."

There was a silent pause. "If Emily talks to the police, we might be next," Mary softly said.

"That's what I'm afraid of," agreed Judy.

It was 4:15 p.m. when Detective Begay arrived at the Surprise Police Department with two warrants. The judge agreed to sign an arrest warrant for the murder of Fred Levine based on the circumstantial evidence and a search warrant on Emily's phone records. Begay met Baxter and Ashford in the Detective Bureau.

It was decided Baxter and Begay would interview Emily while Ashford worked on getting Emily's phone records. Baxter removed Emily from the holding cell and walked her to the secure interview room. Emily remembered the room from the last time she was interrogated. After being read her Miranda rights, Emily agreed to answer questions.

Detective Begay began the questioning. "Emily, I have a warrant for your arrest on the charge of First Degree Murder for Fred Levine's death. We also know Bill was with you when Fred was pushed off the mountain. He followed you and Fred into the park. Here is a security photo of him in his car."

Emily looked at the photo but didn't respond.

"We also have Bill's DNA from the back of Fred's shirt, and the evidence from the mountainside proves he was pushed."

Emily remained silent.

"How long had you been planning this with Bill?"

Emily squinted her eyes and looked at Begay. "We didn't plan anything."

"No one will believe that, Emily. You and Bill planned Fred's death so you and Bill could live together."

"It was an accident," said Emily.

Begay continued. "Bill was struggling with the knowledge he would be arrested once our test results came back. You knew when we arrested Bill, he would crack under the pressure. That's why you hired Chris Molina to shoot Bill. Isn't that right, Emily?"

"That's not true."

"Chris has already told us you hired him," said Baxter. "We interviewed him while you were in the holding cell."

Baxter detected a nervous look on Emily's face.

"And we have multiple interviews of people who you talked to about creating situations to kill their spouses," added Baxter. "I'm sure you had to pay Chris some money upfront before the shooting. What will your bank records tell us?"

Emily was now feeling more nervous. She hadn't thought about the bank records.

"And once we find that down payment, probably in Molina's apartment, we'll find your DNA on the money," said Baxter. "And then, of course, there is your involvement in the killing of Eric Hipple and Jack Kinderman."

"What involvement?" asked Emily.

"Well, you helped plan their killing," said Baxter.

"That's not true. Eric committed suicide, and Jack fell off a ladder."

"That's four homicides," said Begay. "With your cooperation, you can avoid the death penalty."

Emily bowed her head and swallowed. Emily had become accomplished at hiding her emotions, but this statement hit her hard.

"You can avoid that if you just tell us the truth," continued Begay. "You might even work a plea agreement to avoid life without parole."

"I'm sixty-six years old, Detective. Any sentence is a life sentence for me."

"You're not getting out of this, Emily," said Baxter. "It's time to tell the truth and hope for the best. The evidence is overwhelming."

For the first time, the detectives observed raw emotion from Emily. Her eyes welled up with tears.

"Don't hold it in, Emily. It will destroy you," said Baxter.

"May I have some water?"

"Yes," said Begay as he handed Emily a bottle of water.

Emily took a large drink and then said, "First of all, I had nothing to do with the deaths of Eric or Jack. And I can tell you with confidence that neither Mary nor Judy killed their husbands. They are two of the sweetest, least violent women I've known. The fact that both husbands died within days of each other is strictly a coincidence. Any talk you've heard of how to kill spouses is rubbish. We all belonged to a murder mystery book club. We talked about the books we've read and the various ways people are murdered in those books."

"Covering up for your friends won't work, Emily," said Baxter.

"I'm not covering up anything. I'm telling you the truth."

Neither Baxter nor Begay believed Emily. However, it was now obvious she wouldn't implicate her friends.

"Tell us how Fred died," said Begay.

"You already know. However, I didn't see it coming. The day we went hiking, I was surprised to see Bill there. He must have come in after us and then followed Fred and I up the trail. I was in front walking when I heard a commotion and then a scream. I looked back and saw Fred tumbling down the side of the cliff. I didn't know Bill had pushed him until you told me about the DNA."

Baxter and Begay looked at each other in disbelief. "That's not how it happened," said Begay. "Do you expect a jury to believe you weren't involved in the murder but moved in with the man who pushed your husband off a cliff?"

"I didn't know he pushed him until you told me about the DNA. I would have never moved in with him had I known that."

"Then why did you hire Chris Molina to murder Bill?" asked Baxter.

"I didn't hire Chris to murder Bill. Chris was just supposed to scare Bill," said Emily.

"Scare him? For what?"

"Bill said if he were arrested, he would say Fred's death was my idea. It was his way of keeping me quiet. I didn't know what to do, so I hired Chris to scare Bill," explained Emily.

"He scared him alright. Chris shot Bill in the chest," said Baxter. "How much did you pay him in total? And remember, we will get your bank records."

Emily hesitated. "Fifty thousand."

"Fifty thousand to just scare Bill?" asked Baxter.

"Well, I thought he was going to pin Fred's death on me. Fifty thousand to stay out of prison was a bargain. I only wanted Chris to threaten Bill to never tell you guys that I had anything to do with Fred's death. He was never supposed to shoot him."

"Chris has already told us you hired him to shoot Bill," said Baxter.

"I don't know what he told you, but I'm telling you the truth."

"No, you're not, Emily. Chris has made you out as the mastermind of all this."

Emily didn't respond.

Baxter continued. "I believe you paid Chris half the money before he shot Bill in cold blood. Once the job was done, you met today to give him the other half. Isn't that true, Emily?"

"No, I loved Bill."

"You loved Bill? People don't kill those they love."

Just then, there was a knock on the interview room door. Baxter got up and opened the door. It was Detective Denise Gibbs. Baxter stepped out of the room.

"What is it?" asked Baxter.

"Have you read all the police reports yet?" asked Gibbs.

"No. I've been too busy. Why?"

"Several men Bill was playing poker with said Bill received a call just before he left. Bill told them his girlfriend had injured herself and needed to go to the hospital. That's why he left the game early."

"Yeah, I knew that. Thanks for the reminder," said Baxter.

Baxter re-entered the interview room and sat down. He looked right at Emily. "Show us the injury you got last night."

"What are you talking about?"

"I'm talking about your phone call just before Bill left the club. You told him you needed to go to the hospital."

Emily's eyes widened. "I didn't call Bill," she said nervously.

"You did, Emily," replied Baxter. "And your phone records will prove it."

"It's obvious you guys don't believe me," cried Emily. "I'm a victim as much as Bill. Chris is trying to screw me over."

"Stop with the fake crying," said Baxter. "Your story is pathetic. It's all going to come crashing down on you. The entire scheme is falling apart while you stick to your lies. It's time to confess your sins, Emily."

"I'm done talking. Get me an attorney."

"Before we do that, we need to see your injury," said Baxter.

"I told you I'm done talking. I want an attorney."

"I'm not asking you more questions. I'm telling you to show me the injury you suffered at home. I don't have to provide you an attorney to collect physical evidence from you. Only if I ask you more questions. Would you prefer we take pictures of your strip search?"

"Strip search? What are you talking about?"

"When they book you into jail, you will be strip searched for any weapons or contraband. At that time, I can have a female officer examine you and take multiple photos of your body to either document an injury or prove you don't have any."

Emily stared at Baxter.

"You don't have an injury, do you?"

"I said I want an attorney," replied Emily.

"Okay, this interview is over," said Baxter.

Begay and Baxter stood and exited the interview room. Baxter asked an officer to take Emily to the jail for booking. "And be sure to have her body fully examined, photos taken of her body, and note any injuries."

"Yes, sir," said the officer.

"Do you believe her?" asked Baxter.

"Hell no," replied Begay. "She's full of crap."

Baxter laughed. "Yeah, she's one hell of a liar. She was no help on the Hipple or Kinderman case either."

"There's not much more we can do today," said Baxter. "We won't have the search warrant for Molina's apartment until tomorrow."

"I agree," said Begay. "Let's call it a night. Should we meet back here at nine?"

"I'll see you then," said Baxter.

Upon returning to the hotel, Mary and Judy watched local news reports of Bill's homicide, Molina's arrest, and Emily's arrest. Both were concerned over the news of Emily's arrest.

"What should we do?" asked Judy.

"I'm thinking of packing my stuff and getting out of Arizona," said Mary. "My plan has always been to move back to Minnesota."

"You can't leave now," replied Judy. "If you leave now, it will look suspicious, like you're running from the police. You need to give it some time."

"I suppose you're right. I'll need to move back into my house soon. I can't live out of a hotel room forever."

"Once the police are done at my house, I'm going to hire a cleaning company to clean and repaint the patio," said Judy. "I'm not sure if I'll keep the house."

"I get it," said Mary. "The first thing I'm doing is getting a new bed. I won't be able to sleep in the bed Eric died in."

Chapter 24

On Saturday, Begay arrived at the Surprise Police Department promptly at nine o'clock in the morning. He met with Baxter in the detective work area.

"Ashford was able to get the phone records from Emily's phone around the time of Levine's death," said Begay. "He's going through them now."

"Molina's phone was a burner phone," said Baxter. "I need access to that phone as well. Gibbs is on her way to have the on-call judge review my affidavit to search Molina's phone and apartment."

"You have all three phones, correct?" asked Begay.

"Yes. I found Bill's at the scene, and we got Emily's and Molina's at the time of their arrest."

"Great," said Begay. "Do you have any coffee around here?"

"Sure. Downstairs in the break room. There's a coffee machine there."

"Do you want a cup?" asked Begay.

"Yeah, I slept very little last night," sighed Baxter.

Begay left to get coffee. Baxter called Gibbs on her cell phone. "Are you with the judge yet?"

"I just got here a few minutes ago. He's reading the affidavit now. I'll call when I have it signed," said Gibbs.

"Thank you, Denise."

Several minutes later, Begay returned with two cups of coffee. "Here you go," he said while handing Baxter a cup.

"Thanks, Lou. So, how do you think the Diamondbacks will do this year?"

"They've got a good team, that's for sure," said Begay. "That new pitcher they just signed will help. I'm looking forward to the season."

"Yeah, me too. We have an excellent chance to make the playoffs. I've already gotten tickets for the Fourth of July game. The kids will like the after-game fireworks."

As Baxter was talking, his cell phone rang. It was Gibbs calling. Baxter answered the phone. "Did you get the warrant?"

"Yes," said Gibbs. "You're free to search the phones and apartment."

"Thank you, Denise."

Baxter turned to Begay. "We're good. We can look at all the phones now."

Baxter handed Molina's burner phone to Begay. "Let's compare the numbers and times of calls."

After about thirty seconds, Baxter said, "Here's one at 9:49 p.m. Thursday night. Emily received a call from an unknown number."

Begay looked through the calls on the burner phone taken from Chris Molina. "I've got it. At that time, Molina made a call to Emily's number."

"Bingo," said Baxter. "Two minutes later, Emily called Bill's number. That had to be Emily telling Bill she needed to go to the hospital. And then fourteen minutes later, Emily received another call from an unknown number."

"Yep, I see it here," said Begay. "The call lasted just under two minutes. That had to be the call made to confirm Bill had been killed."

"I think you're right," agreed Baxter. "I'll get the printout from the phone companies on Monday."

"Do you mind asking for printouts for the two weeks leading up to and after Fred Levine's death?" asked Begay.

"Of course not. I'll get them to you next week."

"Thanks, Dan. Oh, I'm curious. Did your officers find any injuries on Emily?"

Baxter smiled. "No. And we have the photos to prove it. I heard Emily was quite upset over having to be searched and photographed naked."

"I can imagine," said Begay.

"All I have left to do today is search Molina's apartment," said Baxter. "You can go enjoy the rest of your weekend."

"Thanks, but I'd like to stay to help. I'm attached to this case after all the deceit from Emily and Bill."

"I understand," said Baxter. "Have you had breakfast?"

"Just the coffee we just drank."

"Well, I need something to eat before doing anything else. Let me buy you breakfast at Richi's. It's the least I can do for all the help you've been."

Begay grinned. "I'll go for that."

Richi's was a favorite of Baxter's. When they entered the door, Baxter was greeted by a dark-haired waitress named Teresa. "It's been a while, Dan. Where have you been?"

"It's been busy, Teresa. You know, homicides and stuff."

"Yes, I've heard about it on the news. It's terrible."

"It is, but the investigation is going well."

Teresa led both detectives to a booth by the window. After pouring both of them coffee, Teresa took their order. Baxter ordered the Saturday special. Two eggs, bacon, hash browns, and two pancakes. Begay ordered a garden omelet with hash browns and wheat toast.

"No meat today?" asked Baxter.

"Nah, I'm trying to cut back some."

"Yeah, I can see you're getting a little fat."

"Fat? I run three miles most days and lift weights regularly. Would you like to see my abs?" joked Begay.

"No, I'm good," laughed Baxter.

"I've lost ten pounds over the last three months," said Begay.

"I was joking. You look great."

Begay smiled. "I'll race you back to the P.D."

"Next time," smiled Baxter.

Neither detective talked about the case while eating breakfast. Most of the talk centered on the start of baseball's spring training. They also debated whether the Phoenix Suns would make the playoffs.

Once they had finished breakfast, Baxter paid the bill, then drove them to Molina's apartment complex in El Mirage, a small city on the east side of Surprise. Gibbs met them in the parking lot. Molina's apartment was on the second level of an old three-floor brick building of twenty-four apartments. The door to Molina's apartment was weathered. All three detectives entered using the key they had gotten from Molina.

The apartment was dimly lit. Heavy drapes hung from two windows looking out onto the parking lot. The apartment was reasonably clean but messy. Several beer cans were on the living room table, and the room smelled of old cigarette smoke.

"I'll take the living room and kitchen if you two take the bedrooms," said Baxter.

"Will do," said Gibbs.

Baxter began inspecting the room. A black hooded sweatshirt was hanging on the back of one of the kitchen chairs. Baxter carefully placed it in a brown paper bag and sealed it with evidence tape. Nothing else of evidentiary value was in plain sight. Baxter looked through all the kitchen drawers and cabinets. He then heard a shout from the main bedroom.

"Found it!" shouted Gibbs.

Baxter walked down the short hallway to the bedroom. Gibbs had a black canvas gym bag lying on top of the bed. The top was open, and she was looking inside. She then held up several bundles of one-hundred-dollar bills in her gloved right hand and showed them to Begay and Baxter.

Baxter smiled. "You found the down payment."

"That's not all," said Begay. "We found a partial box of forty caliber hollow point bullets in the bottom dresser drawer."

"Molina is screwed," replied Baxter.

The detectives finished their search, bagged up the evidence they found, and then locked the front door on their way out. Baxter dropped Begay off at his car in the police parking lot.

"Thanks for your help today, Lou."

"And thank you for your help in solving Fred's murder," replied Begay. "Are you coming in tomorrow?"

"No. I'm going to take Sunday off and spend it with my family. It's been a long week, and nothing will happen tomorrow. On Monday, I'll take another shot at interviewing Molina in the morning before he is assigned an attorney. With this additional evidence, I think I can get him to turn on Emily."

"Would you like me to help?" asked Begay.

"No, I'll have Gibbs help me. We'll see how Molina responds to a woman. After that, I'm setting my sights on Mary and Judy."

"Alright. Good luck, and have an enjoyable day off, Dan."

"Same to you, Lou."

Meanwhile, news of Bill's murder and the arrest of Emily Settlemire and Chris Molina was on all the local news channels. A Facebook group was created by a Cactus View resident for those who wanted to discuss the case. The group had only been up for about six hours but already had two-hundred-twenty-three subscribers. The book club was now being referred to as the Murderer's Club. One poster went so far as to post a photograph of Linda's husband, Ray, playing pickleball. The post referred to Ray as the husband of the Murderer's Club leader.

Linda had already been interviewed by four local news stations. She tried to convince the reporters the club had nothing to do with murder or condoning murder as a way to get rid of husbands. Ray finally shut down their cell phones when reporters continued to call with questions.

The other club members also received calls from reporters hoping to get an admission or juicy quote to use in their stories. The only one who would talk to them was Katy. She agreed to speak with one reporter on camera. A reporter and cameraman came to Katy's house at four-thirty Saturday afternoon. Katy wore one of her favorite dresses for the interview. It was a blue-printed, casual V-neck dress with short sleeves.

When the reporter and cameraman arrived, they wanted the interview staged on Katy's front patio with her back to the house. After several innocuous questions about the club and how it started, the reporter asked heavier questions.

Reporter: "How did the book club become a club of, should we say, murder enthusiasts?"

"Not all of us," said Katy. "When Emily Settlemire came into the club, everything seemed to change. Conversations turned into ways to kill your spouse."

Reporter: "What were some of the suggestions Emily talked about?"

"She talked generally about accidents and illnesses, but never talked about specifics."

Reporter: "And this was something your membership supported?"

"I certainly didn't. But I believe some did."

Reporter: "Are you talking about Judy Kinderman and Mary Hipple?"

While Katy suspected Judy and Mary of being involved in their husband's deaths, she wasn't comfortable accusing them of murder on TV.

"I'm not sure," said Katy.

Reporter: "You just said some members supported murder. Please tell us who supported murder as a way to get out of a marriage?."

Katy felt trapped. With a reporter and TV camera in her face, she hesitated to accuse Judy and Mary. The reporter could see Katy was uncomfortable. Katy tried to walk back her statement.

"I don't know if anyone actually supported it. It was just discussed within the group," said Katy.

Reporter: "Katy, you have told others you believe Judy Kinderman and Mary Hipple were involved in their husband's deaths. Are you rescinding those comments?"

"I, uh, don't know," stuttered Katy. "They could be, but the police haven't arrested them."

Reporter: "But their husbands both died under strange circumstances. After discussing ways to get away with murder, don't you believe they followed Emily's script?"

"Um, I don't know. It's possible," admitted Katy.

Reporter: "Alright, Katy. Thank you for sharing with us today. For more breaking news on this incredible story about a women's book club that may have been promoting murder, stay tuned for updates as they come in."

After Katy's interview appeared on the six o'clock news, she was inundated with calls from other reporters wanting to get an interview. Katy let the calls go to voice messaging.

Katy's husband, Jerry, was not happy with Katy. "I told you not to do the interview. Now look what we're dealing with."

"I just told them the truth," replied Katy.

"You need to be careful, Katy. You could get us sued."

"For what? I told the truth."

"No, you said what you think might be true. You don't really know."

"I know," said Katy. "But don't worry. I'm not doing any more TV interviews."

Judy's phone rang. It was Maritza Perez calling. "Hello, Maritza."

"How are you doing, Judy?"

"Okay, given the circumstances."

"I've seen the news, and I heard about your interview with the police."

"What did you hear?"

"That you're afraid the police will charge you with murder."

"I didn't murder my husband, Maritza."

"I believe you, Judy, but you need an attorney, and Ricardo has offered to represent you."

"Won't that make me look guilty?"

"People being investigated need attorneys to help them through the investigative process."

"I didn't know Ricardo had criminal experience."

"Not a lot," said Maritza, "but he has some. He can at least be with you if you get interviewed again. It would be nice to have an advocate for your benefit."

"I thought you wanted nothing to do with me," said Judy.

"Well, I certainly didn't care for the nature of our book club conversations, but that doesn't mean I no longer care about you. Why don't you come over and just talk with Ricardo? He has tomorrow afternoon free. He can meet with you at one o'clock."

"He's okay with that?"

"Yes. He told me to call you."

"Well, I suppose it can't hurt."

"Good. I'll see you tomorrow around one."

"Yes, I'll be there," said Judy.

Chapter 25

On Sunday afternoon, Judy arrived at the Perez residence, as expected. Both Maritza and Ricardo met her at the door.

"Come on in," said Maritza.

"Hi, Judy," said Ricardo. "Our third bedroom is our office. Why don't we go meet in there?"

"Would you like something to drink?" asked Maritza.

"No, thank you."

Ricardo led Judy to his makeshift office. He sat at a desk covered in paperwork. Judy sat in a cushioned folding chair facing the desk.

"I've done some criminal work during my career, but never anything like a homicide," explained Ricardo. "Most of my work was in corporate law. However, the concepts of any criminal defense are generally the same. Maritza told me of your situation, so I thought I'd offer assistance during the investigation. But I must say to you, if you get charged with homicide, I will need to recuse myself. You will need an attorney who specializes in serious criminal cases. Do you understand?"

"Yes," said Judy.

"Given those conditions, would you like my help through the investigation?"

"I could use some help," admitted Judy.

"Okay. The first thing I need to know is everything that happened the day you found Jack on the patio."

Judy hesitated as she pondered whether to tell the absolute truth. Only Mary and Judy knew what really happened.

"Start with what happened when you arrived home," said Ricardo.

"Okay. Do you know Jack was cheating on me?"

"Yes, I understand that's why you moved out."

"I had moved out because I decided to seek a divorce. I was staying in the hotel and needed to return home to get some of my things. I arrived that afternoon and couldn't find Jack. When I walked around to the back patio, I saw him lying there. Paint was spilled all over, and the ladder was lying across his body. He had been painting the house, and it was apparent he had fallen. Blood was running from the back of his head and out of his mouth. It was an awful scene. I rushed over to him, pulled the ladder off of him, and checked his breathing. He wasn't breathing, so I called nine-one-one. The dispatcher directed me to check for his pulse. I couldn't find one."

"Why do the police think you had something to do with his fall?" asked Ricardo.

"They found my fingerprints on the ladder. They also found blood and splashed paint on my pants. I guess they think this is evidence I killed Jack."

"You would have gotten all that from checking on Jack."

"That's what I told the detective. He said something about the paint being spatter. I don't know what that means."

"Generally, it means a liquid, such as blood or paint, was transferred to another object at a higher velocity. Did you step in the paint?"

"I'm sure I did. It was everywhere."

"Maybe you were excited and ran or jumped in the paint?"

Judy hadn't done that, but she agreed anyway. "Yes, I think I did."

"That could be an explanation," said Ricardo. "But stepping or jumping in the paint would have splashed away from your legs, not toward your legs."

"The detective was also concerned with how wet the blood and paint were when police arrived," said Judy.

"The degree of wet or dryness could help determine a time of death," said Ricardo. "If the paint and blood were wet, his fall probably happened just before your arrival."

"Yeah, maybe," said Judy.

"Tell me about your discussions on ways to kill your spouses?"

Judy didn't know what to say. Several seconds passed.

"Maritza told me about some of the discussions at book club with Emily. It's no secret, Judy. And Katy certainly believes you staged the accident. She also believes you and Mary met with Emily to discuss killing your husbands. I'm sure the police have this information as well."

"The only discussions about murder that I've had are with book club members, and they were regarding the books we've read," explained Judy.

"Well, I know Maritza was uncomfortable with the discussions. In any case, it is something the police will consider."

"Yes, the detective already questioned me about it," said Judy.

Ricardo paused for several seconds before continuing. "The unfortunate circumstance is you arrived just after Jack had fallen."

"Why is that unfortunate?" asked Judy.

"Well, the paint spatter on your clothing is evidence that may be hard to explain. Simply walking or running through the crime scene would not have caused the tiny paint spatters on your pants. At least, that's what an expert might testify to. I wasn't there, so I can't explain it either. However, had you gotten there before he fell, the paint spilled onto the patio would have sent large and tiny spatters of paint in all directions."

"The police would then think I pushed him off the ladder," said Judy.

"Yeah, maybe you're right," said Ricardo. "But I'm assuming you didn't knock him off the ladder. Had you gotten there earlier while Jack was still alive, he may have been angry to see you. Maybe an argument would have ensued, and Jack, getting upset, might have lost his balance and fell as you stood there watching in horror."

Judy wasn't sure whether Ricardo was fictionalizing the event, whether he didn't believe her version, or whether he was suggesting a different type of lie.

"Why are you telling me this, Ricardo?"

"Because I think you might be lying about what happened, Judy. And I'd hate to see the lie used against you in court."

Judy swallowed, not knowing how to respond. She could feel her right leg shaking as it usually did when she was nervous. Her skin felt clammy.

"As your attorney, whatever you tell me is privileged information. I can never be called to testify against you."

Judy thought for a moment. "No matter what I tell you?"

"No matter what you tell me, Judy."

Judy shook as she muttered, "Yes, I was there when Jack fell."

Ricardo leaned back in his chair. "Tell me what happened, Judy."

Judy took a deep breath. "I returned to the house to get some of my things. I was going to leave Jack, and he was angry about it. At first, I didn't see him. Then I heard some noise from the back patio. When I walked around to the patio, I saw Jack on the extension ladder painting the peak of the house. I was surprised to see him up there so high. I told him I was just there to get some of my belongings. He was not happy to see me and started yelling at me. Jack told me I couldn't go into the house until he was done painting. Of course, this made me angry, and I yelled back that it was my house, too. This only made him angrier. I remember seeing him twisting on the ladder to look at me as he yelled. The next thing I knew, he lost his balance and fell. There was a horrible thud on the patio. I could hear his head hit the pavement."

Judy wiped tears from her eyes before continuing.

"Paint went flying everywhere, and the ladder came down on Jack. When I saw blood coming from the back of Jack's head, I moved the ladder off of him to render him aid. When I saw he was unconscious, I called 911."

"That would explain the paint spatters," said Ricardo. "It would also explain why the paint and blood were still wet when the police arrived. It doesn't explain the talk of killing your husband."

"But I told you, the talk was about stories from the books we've read."

"Others may testify differently, Judy. Especially Katy. That's not insurmountable, but it will be a problem if you are ever charged."

"Do you think I'll be charged with murder?" asked Judy.

"I don't know. It will depend on whether the police believe your new account of events. Or maybe they have evidence to challenge your story."

"Do you believe me?" asked Judy.

"It doesn't matter what I believe. It only matters what the police and/or a jury believes."

"What's the next step?" asked Judy.

"I'll set up a new interview with the detective so that you can tell him what you just told me."

"I have to talk to him again?" asked Judy.

"Yes. You need to tell him what you just told me."

Judy nodded as tears ran down her cheeks. "I'm sorry, Ricardo."

"What are you sorry for?"

"Just this whole big mess. I never wanted it to happen like this."

"No one ever does. Why don't you get some rest today? I'll let you know when the interview is set," said Ricardo.

"Okay, thank you."

After Judy left, Maritza asked Ricardo if Judy had killed Jack.

"You know I can't tell you that, but off the record, I don't really know for sure."

"Is she going to be charged with murder?"

"I don't know that either, but if she sticks to her story, it may be hard to convict her."

While Judy was meeting with Ricardo, Linda called the remaining book club members to let them know she would no longer host the book club. The news coverage and intense community backlash on social media had worn her out. She hoped that some community attention would dissolve by disbanding the club. Whether or not it did, Linda no longer wanted to continue. Once all members had been notified and a message left for Judy, Linda and her husband, Ray, crafted a written statement for all local media outlets. The statement read:

It is with sadness that I announce the disbanding of the Cactus View Book Club. The attention brought upon the club by the unlawful and immoral actions of one of our members has harmed the purpose and integrity of the book club. For that, I am sorry. We support the police investigation into the murders of Fred Levine and Bill Hutchins. Like others, we grieve their untimely deaths. I am hoping the disbanding of our book club will relieve community concerns as well.

This will be my last statement on these matters. Please do not call or come to our house. I will not answer any further questions.

Linda Riggs

Chapter 26

It was 9:35 a.m. on Monday morning, and Detectives Baxter and Begay had just finished meeting with the District Attorney. After much discussion, it was decided to charge 23-year-old Chris Molina with Conspiracy to Commit Murder, First Degree Murder, and Robbery. Emily Settlemire was to be charged with two counts of Conspiracy to Commit Murder and two counts of First Degree Murder for the deaths of Fred Levine and Bill Hutchins. First appearances for both suspects were scheduled for later in the afternoon.

Detective Denise Gibbs was waiting for Baxter when he returned to the detective bureau.

"Everything go okay with the D.A.?" asked Gibbs.

"Yes. Now we need to pull Chris back in here and get him to turn on Emily. Her case is the weakest. I have two officers escorting him over."

"The interview room is ready to go," said Gibbs.

When Molina arrived, he was placed in the interview room. Baxter allowed him to sit alone for fifteen minutes.

"Making suspects wait adds stress," explained Baxter. "It gives them time to wonder what we'll ask them."

"Doesn't he have an attorney?" asked Gibbs.

"Not yet. He'll be assigned one at his hearing today. That's why I wanted to get him in here before then."

Baxter and Gibbs walked into the room together. Gibbs handed Molina a bottle of water.

"I've already answered your questions," said Molina.

"We know, Chris," said Baxter. "We thought you'd want an update on what we have. Do you mind?"

Molina frowned. "What do you have?"

"You were advised of your Miranda Rights last week. Those still apply. Do you understand that?"

"Yes."

"Good," said Baxter. "You should know we found the other half of your payout from Emily in your apartment. We also found your bullets, which will undoubtedly match your Glock handgun and the bullets removed from Bill Hutchins' chest."

Baxter noticed Molina nervously shifting in his chair.

"Oh, and we found the phone calls between you and Emily on your burner phone. The calls aligned nicely with the time of the shooting."

Molina turned his head to the side.

"Look at me, Chris," demanded Baxter. "The kicker is that Emily told us you were paid to only scare Bill into not talking to the police."

Molina turned his head and looked directly at Baxter with a furrowed brow.

"That's right, Chris. Emily is ready to testify you acted on your own in killing Bill. We have nothing to prove her wrong."

"You're lying," said Molina.

"Denise, show Chris the highlighted report," said Baxter.

Gibbs slid a report page from a stack of papers. "I've highlighted her statement for you," said Gibbs as she handed Molina the page.

Molina read the highlighted section.

"That's an official police report, Chris," said Baxter. "Look at the top of it."

Molina took a deep breath. "She's lying."

"What is she lying about, Chris?"

"That bitch hired me to kill her boyfriend because she was afraid he was going to confess everything to the police. I will not take the fall for this myself. I'll testify against her if I have to."

"You're admitting then that you were hired to kill Bill Hutchins?"

"That's what the money was for," said Molina.

"And you did what she paid you to do, correct?"

"I said that's what the money was for. I'm done talking now. Just make sure that bitch gets what's coming to her."

"We will," said Baxter. "I have one more question that has nothing to do with you. I hope you'll answer it. Did Emily ever admit that she convinced Bill to push Fred off the mountain?"

After several seconds, Molina answered. "Yeah. She and Bill were in on it. Although it took a lot of convincing to get Bill to go along. When he started to panic about the investigation, she called me."

"Thank you, Chris."

Baxter called for an officer to take Molina back to jail. When he and Gibbs returned to the bureau, they whooped and high-fived each other.

"We now have a solid case," said Baxter. "Thank you for the help, Denise."

"My pleasure. It was fun, and I learned a lot."

"Two down and two to go," said Baxter.

"I'm surprised how all of this emanated from a quiet retirement community. Affairs, abuse, conspiracies, murder, who knew?" said Gibbs.

"It's not always like this," said Baxter. "They're usually too busy playing softball, golf, pickleball, or whatever."

"Whatever? You mean like murderous book clubs?"

"Yeah, that too," laughed Baxter. "I've got to call Lou with an update on today's interview. He'll be happy to know Molina pointed the finger at Emily in Fred's death. It strengthens his case."

Before he called Detective Begay with the news, Baxter noticed he had a message on his phone. He opened the message and listened. It was from attorney Ricardo Perez requesting another interview with his client, Judy Kinderman. Baxter was puzzled but curious as to what Judy had to say. He called Perez back and arranged an interview at two o'clock that afternoon.

"Hey, Denise," called out Baxter. "Would you be available to cover the appearance in court today? Judy Kinderman is coming in for an interview at two o'clock."

"Sure, no problem," said Gibbs. "Are you going to get another confession?"

"I doubt it. She's coming in with an attorney."

Waiting for two o'clock to arrive seemed to take forever for Judy. She was a bundle of nerves, unable to eat or relax. Judy had confided in Mary the night before. They were having lunch at Panera's prior to Judy's scheduled interview. Judy had hardly touched her salad.

"Are you sure this is the right thing to do?" Mary asked.

"No, but Ricardo thinks I have a better chance of acquittal if I admit I was there when Jack fell. It's all because of the damn paint spatter and my fingerprints. I never even heard of spatter before. Oh, and because of Katy's big mouth."

"I don't want to see you go to jail, Judy. If you admit you were there, Detective Baxter may arrest you."

Judy teared up. "That's what I'm afraid of, Mary."

"Not to add to your stress, but there's something I'm nervous about as well," said Mary.

"What is it?"

Mary hesitated.

"It's okay," said Judy. "You can tell me."

"I know how the police try to make deals with people to get them to talk."

"Yeah, I understand that," said Judy.

"Well," said Mary, "I'm afraid Baxter may offer you a deal to tell the truth about me."

"Oh, my god, Mary. I would never say anything about you and Eric."

"People are constantly pressured to expose friends in police interviews," said Mary.

"I promise I will not admit to knowing anything about Eric's suicide," Judy assured her.

Mary nodded. "Thank you. Sorry, but I had to ask."

"I understand," said Judy.

It was 2:05 p.m. when Ricardo Perez arrived at the Surprise Police Department with his client, Judy Kinderman. Ricardo introduced himself to Detective Baxter.

"I was thinking you changed your mind," said Baxter.

"No. Traffic on Bell was worse than I expected. There must be a spring training game today," said Ricardo.

Baxter led them both to the interview room. Two bottles of water were already waiting for them at the table. Baxter had Ricardo and Judy sit across from him.

"What can I do for you?" asked Baxter.

"Judy would like to amend her statement," said Ricardo.

"Go ahead. I'm listening."

Ricardo nodded to Judy. She took a deep breath, then began.

"I lied earlier when I said I hadn't witnessed Jack falling from the ladder. When I arrived, I found him on the ladder, painting the back of the house. Jack was upset to see me there. I told him I was there to pick up some personal items, but he didn't want me to go into the house without him. Jack told me to wait until he finished painting. I argued the house was as much mine as his. He then said I had given up my right to the house by leaving. I can't even remember everything we said, but we were screaming at each other. Jack became animated and was pointing a finger at me. Suddenly, he lost his balance and fell to the patio. The ladder then came crashing down onto him. He made a terrible thud as he hit the pavement, and paint spilled all over, splashing paint onto my pants. I was stunned at first. Then, I saw blood oozing out from behind his head, and he was making gurgling sounds. Bubbles and blood came out of Jack's mouth. I stepped forward, grabbed onto the ladder, and pulled it off of Jack. I then called 9-1-1."

Baxter stared at Judy for several seconds before saying, "That's an incredible story. Did your attorney help you with that?"

"That question is inappropriate," said Ricardo. "If you have any legitimate questions, ask them. Otherwise, we can leave."

"Well," said Baxter, "that's not what Judy told me the last time we talked. Why should I believe you now, Judy?"

"I was afraid the last time we talked. I knew about some things Katy had said, and I knew Eric had just committed suicide. I was afraid you wouldn't believe me."

"You could have just as easily pulled that ladder out from under Jack," said Baxter. "That's why your fingerprints are on it."

Judy was crying. "Yes, but I didn't do that. I'm telling you the truth. I pulled the ladder off of him."

"Emily told you how to stage accidents. That's what you did, and now you want me to believe you had nothing to do with it?"

"I lied before because I was afraid," insisted Judy. "I'm not afraid to tell the truth now."

"That, or you're telling me a new lie," said Baxter.

"Do you have any more questions for my client?" asked Ricardo.

Baxter looked at Ricardo, then back at Judy. "Yeah, I do. If Jack fell from atop the ladder, it would be logical for the top of the ladder to fall on Jack. Why would you go to the bottom of the ladder to move it?"

Judy thought for a moment. "Things happened so fast I can't remember all the details. I just grabbed the closest part of the ladder to move it. That's all I remember."

"Judy," said Baxter, "I can help you lessen the time you would serve if you simply tell the truth. No jury will believe that between you, Mary, and Emily, three men have accidentally died, and a fourth was gunned down in cold blood without your planning and conspiracy to kill. Tell me everything, and you will become a prime witness in three murders. Your valued testimony will result in a minimal charge and sentence for your cooperation."

"But, I have cooperated," said Judy.

"I want the truth, Judy. I can call someone from the District Attorney's Office if you're willing to negotiate a deal."

"Detective, give me a few minutes to confer with my client," said Ricardo.

Baxter reached over to shut off the recording equipment. "Let me know when you're finished by pressing the buzzer," said Baxter as he left the room.

Once Baxter left, Ricardo asked Judy if she wanted him to negotiate a deal.

"No," said Judy. "I haven't killed anyone or helped anyone else."

"If they get someone else to talk and it's not in your favor, you could be charged with homicide. Then you'll have no other cards to play."

Judy thought for several seconds. She finally said, "I don't know anything about the other deaths. I have nothing more to say."

"Okay, Judy, I just wanted to be sure."

"I'm sure," said Judy.

Ricardo pressed the buzzer. Baxter re-entered the room.

"What's it going to be?" asked Baxter.

"Judy has nothing more to say, Detective."

Baxter shook his head. "Okay, I'll forward your statement to the D.A.'s office."

Ricardo and Judy stood up to leave. "Thank you for your time," said Ricardo.

After they had left, Baxter walked back to his desk and slammed down his file folder.

"What's wrong?" asked Detective Gibbs.

"Judy and her lawyer friend may have outfoxed us."

"How so?"

"I think her lawyer, Ricardo Perez, the husband of book club member Maritza Perez, talked Judy into admitting she was at the crime scene to help explain the evidence. She now says she was present when Jack accidentally fell off the ladder."

"Do you have enough to charge her?" asked Gibbs.

"I'll take what I have to the District Attorney to see if she believes there is enough evidence to convict her."

"Do you believe there is?"

"Honestly, I think it would be hard to convince a jury. Judy can come across as very credible. They would also sympathize with her about Jack's cheating lifestyle."

"What about the other one, Mary Hipple?"

"Same deal. Some things just don't make sense. Why would Mary's husband get naked to commit suicide? And why would he crush the sleeping pills into his drink when he could have easily just swallowed the pills?"

"Are you going to bring Mary in for another interview?"

"I don't think it would do much good. I don't have enough leverage on Mary. However, the circumstances surrounding the book club and conversations about staging accidents and illnesses are too coincidental for my comfort. But I'll present what I have to the D.A. to see what she thinks about pressing charges. There's still one person left who could break it wide open."

"Who's that?"

"Emily Settlemire. She's the one stirring the pot, and now that she is facing two murder charges, she may be more willing to help herself by telling us what she knows. Which reminds me, how did it go at the first appearances?"

"Very well. The judge bound both of them over on murder and conspiracy charges. Emily was charged with two counts of conspiracy and two counts of murder. Molina was charged with conspiracy, murder, and robbery. Detective Begay was very pleased."

Baxter smiled. "I'm sure he was. That was a tough case."

Chapter 27

On Wednesday, Baxter met District Attorney Cathy Stewart in her office to discuss the deaths of Eric Hipple and Jack Kinderman. Baxter laid out the details and evidence of each case, including the alleged conversations of staging accidents or illnesses to kill spouses. Baxter described each member of the Cactus View Book Club. He then reviewed the statements given by each member.

"You present an interesting case," said Stewart. "Some of it is hearsay, of course, but Katy Cullen provides the strongest testimony to the alleged conversations. Other members seem to be holding back or covering for each other."

"That's what makes these cases so complex," said Baxter. "Much of the conversation involved innuendos and speculation. But Emily planted ideas into the heads of these women. Judy and Mary met with Emily on at least two occasions."

"Do you have proof of what they were discussing?" asked Stewart.

"No. But I have a witness. Emily Settlemire. If we can get her to talk, I might get enough to charge both women. This is where I need your help."

"You want me to offer Settlemire a deal to break her silence, correct?"

"Yes."

"I don't have a lot of wiggle room on first-degree homicide charges. And Emily committed two homicides. What are you thinking I should offer?"

"You could take the death penalty off the table," said Baxter.

"We won't go for that anyway. She's sixty-six years old."

"Yeah, even Emily pointed that out," agreed Baxter. "What about a sentence that gives her a chance to be out before she dies?"

"On two counts of First Degree Murder?"

"Yeah, I know," said Baxter. "I didn't think you'd go for that. What if I lie to her? I could tell her you have agreed to only ask for twenty years if she tells us the truth. She might think if she lived another twenty years, she would have a couple years of freedom in her final years."

"You'd never be able to use it in court. Any judge would throw out the testimony for coercing her with a false deal."

"Yes, but if she tells us what I believe she knows, I will have it recorded. I could then play it for Mary and Judy to make them think we have admissible evidence. We could then offer them a deal if they tell the truth."

"So long as they plead guilty. A judge would probably throw the confessions out," said Stewart.

"If you made the deal sweet enough, they might take it. Otherwise, we have nothing."

"Depending on the judge, if he or she learned of the deception, the entire case might be thrown out."

"It's not a deception if Emily tells the truth," argued Baxter. "I only want to play her statement for our suspects to hear. I won't say that Emily will testify. But if they infer that, then they might talk."

"You make a good argument," agreed Stewart. "But I can't be part of offering Emily a deal. There would be an official record of that. If you want to lie to Emily about a potential deal, that's your business."

"What else do we have? Neither will confess unless we have something to pressure them with. The courts have upheld deception so long as it's not coercive enough to make an innocent person confess to something they didn't do."

"Yes, I know the law, Dan."

"So, what do you think?"

"You do what you believe is necessary to solve your cases. Just make sure it's legal."

"Thank you, Cathy."

The following day, Thursday, Baxter arranged an interview with Emily Settlemire and her attorney at the county jail. He explained that whatever she said would not and could not be used against her. He also hinted that her testimony about Judy and Mary would go a long way toward getting a reduced sentence.

Emily was escorted from her jail cell to a concrete block-walled room used for interviews. She wore an orange jumpsuit with Maricopa County Jail emblazoned in bold black letters across the back. Her shoulder-length highlighted brown hair wasn't as neatly combed as before. Her attorney, Max Windell, with his long gray hair and bushy eyebrows, reminded Baxter of Albert Einstein.

"What exactly is this interview for, Detective?" asked Windell.

"As I said over the phone, it is to ask questions about the deaths of Eric Hipple and Jack Kinderman. I will not ask Emily questions about her cases. If she cooperates, the D.A. will consider a reduced sentence."

"How much of a reduction?" asked Windell.

"It all depends on how much Emily tells me today."

"Alright, you may ask your questions. But I will stop you if it may compromise my client's case."

"I understand," said Baxter. "Nothing she says today can be used against her. Here is the agreement with my signature on it."

Windell looked it over. "Okay, you may begin."

"Emily, I'd like to ask you about your conversations with Mary and Judy over the last month or so. I understand there were some conversations about staging accidents and illnesses."

"Where did you hear that?" asked Emily.

"From talking to many people. Some of it is hearsay or secondhand, but I believe you were directly involved in some of those conversations."

"Mary and Judy are friends of mine. We had lots of conversations."

"Yes, and I understand some of them involved ways to get rid of your husbands."

"Yes, they did."

Finally, thought Baxter. Emily's going to give him what he needs. "Can you elaborate on what those ways were?"

"Sure. We talked about just packing their bags and leaving. Mary had an abusive husband and wanted to move back to Minnesota. Judy's husband cheated on her non-stop. I told her to leave him. Move back to Washington. No one needs to put up with that crap. They needed to leave and file for divorce."

"Yes, but you also talked about how to get rid of husbands through staged accidents or illnesses," said Baxter.

"What are you talking about?" asked Emily.

"Emily, now is your time to help yourself by telling the truth. I know you talked about staging accidents."

"Where did you get this nonsense?" asked Emily. "If you are going by what crazy Katy told you, then you've been had."

"You won't help yourself by telling me the truth?"

Emily smirked. "I told you before, I'm already sixty-six years old, Detective. There isn't a deal the D.A. could give me to save me a life sentence. I have a better chance of being found not guilty than playing this game."

Baxter knew she was right. Nothing he could say would change her mind. Whatever secrets Emily knew, she was taking them to prison with her.

"Alright, Emily. I understand your position. I appreciate you at least hearing me out."

With that, the interview and Detective Baxter's investigations were over. Absent Mary or Judy wanting to relieve a guilty heart, there was nothing else for Baxter to do.

When Baxter returned to the police department, he found two forensic reports on his desk. According to the findings of the first report, the intact bullet taken from Bill Hutchins' chest was fired from the Glock forty caliber handgun recovered from Chris Molina at the time of his arrest. In the second report, DNA from Emily Settlemire matched swabs from some of the money found in Molina's apartment. Baxter smiled, knowing neither Emily nor Chris would ever see freedom again.

Detective Gibbs walked in and saw Baxter at his desk. "How did the interview with Emily go?" asked Gibbs.

"She held to her story. She wouldn't turn on her friends."

"You must be pretty disappointed," said Gibbs.

"Surprisingly, I'm not."

"I thought you wanted to get the other two ladies for murder?"

"I did, and I gave it my best shot. But there's a part of me that's okay with it."

"Why is that?" asked Gibbs.

"Well, they both had assholes for husbands. Their friends told me how abusive their husbands had been. In Mary's case, she was physically and emotionally abused for most of the marriage. Did you know that her husband once threatened to kill her and bury her under concrete?"

"No, I hadn't heard that," said Gibbs.

"Can you imagine the fear she lived with? I actually felt sorry for her. The abuse may have been enough to justify killing her husband. He also controlled all the money, leaving her no way out."

"You still don't think he committed suicide?" asked Gibbs.

"It's possible, but he wasn't the type. He would have killed Mary before he took his own life."

"I can see that," said Gibbs. "What about Judy with the ladder story?"

"Not quite the same, but her husband cheated on her almost the entire time they were married. Now, most women would simply divorce a husband like that, but he also controlled the finances. He was a big-time surgeon and would have made life hell for Judy."

"I understand why you're okay with this," said Gibbs.

"Denise, this job is not always black and white. Sometimes, people go to jail for doing what most of us might do in a similar situation. In these two instances, the women weren't the bad guys. It was my job to do my best, but deep down, I was pleased when Emily stuck to her story. She's accepting what she deserves without taking the others with her."

"Do you feel sorry for Emily?" asked Gibbs.

"Oh, hell no. Emily is pure evil. She's like the black widow, as Katy would say. If we could go back and exhume the body of her second husband, I'll bet we would find he was drugged in some manner. And what she did to Bill is unconscionable. She suckered him into helping her murder Fred, and then she had Bill brutally shot. I hope she rots in hell."

Gibbs nodded. "I agree."

Conclusion

Five Months Later

Neither Mary nor Judy were charged with any crime. Mary moved back to Minnesota and lived with one of her sons. She had been able to regularly visit her mother until her mother's death six weeks prior. After no charges were filed, the life insurance company had to pay Mary two million dollars from Eric's life insurance policy. Mary also hired an attorney to fight for access to Eric's money. She was also fighting for ownership of her home in Cactus View. Her lawyer filed a lawsuit against Eric's brother, claiming Mary's marriage to Eric granted her at least half ownership of the house. While her attorney wasn't sure they could get half ownership, he hoped the outlook of a drawn-out legal battle would prompt the brother to settle by giving Mary half of the house's value. The now-vacant Cactus View house was not being used.

Judy remained in her home in Cactus View. With no one to challenge her access to Jack's fortune, Judy became a wealthy widow. She sold their mortgage-free home in

Washington for one million five hundred thousand dollars. Once she knew she wouldn't be charged, Judy kept a low profile for several months. After the attention and rumors subsided, Judy became more involved in the activities offered by the Cactus View community.

The Cactus View Book Club disbanded after Emily's arrest. The community and media attention on the club was too much for the remaining members to stomach. However, after six months, Linda decided to re-establish the club. She invited the previous members still in the community to join a newer version of their book club. Linda personally met with Judy to convince her to join, but she declined to rejoin the club.

The first meeting was held during the first week of September. The new group was composed of three original members and four new members. The first order of business was to make introductions.

Linda Riggs started with an introduction and explanation of the book club. While it would include crime novels, the club was expanding into other genres to add more variety.

After Linda, Maritza Perez, and Katy Cullen each introduced themselves. Linda then turned to the new members. Talia Williams was the first African American to join the book club.

"Talia, why don't you go first?"

"Thank you," said Talia. "I'm Talia Williams. I'm sixty-six years old, and I'm married to Robert Williams. I'm a retired hospital administrator. We have two grown boys, and we recently moved to Cactus View. I'm looking forward to making friends and reading good books."

"How long have you been married?" asked Katy.

"We've been married thirty-six years."

"Do you have a good marriage?"

"Yes. Why would you ask me that?"

"Just curious," said Katy.

Next, it was Teresa Phillip's turn.

"My name is Teresa Phillips. I'm sixty-nine years old, divorced, and have three children. I have a son and two girls. I've been in Cactus View for three years now, and when I met Linda at the rec center, she convinced me to join the group. Thank you for having me. I enjoy reading and discussing books with others."

"Any grandchildren?" asked Linda.

"Yes. I have seven grandchildren."

Next, it was Becky Miller's turn.

"Hello, everyone. I'm Becky Miller. I'm seventy and have been married to my husband Bob for forty-six years. We have five grown children and eight grandchildren so far. One of my other hobbies is painting. I have lived in Cactus View for six years. And before anyone asks, yes, my husband and I are happily married."

Finally, it was Sue Myers' turn. "Hi, I'm Sue Myers. I'm seventy-one years old and currently single. I have had two husbands but no children. My spouses and I were always too busy for children. I recently moved to Cactus View for all the activities and to make new friends. I enjoy hikes in the local mountain parks. I joined this club because I enjoy reading and need to make new friends."

"May I ask what happened to your two husbands?" asked Katy.

"I've had bad luck with spouses," said Sue. "I've outlived both of them. My first one became very ill and died. My second husband was killed in a horrible boating accident."

Katy's eyes grew large, and she looked directly at Linda.

Linda could see that Maritza was also looking at her with a "what the hell?" look.

Linda raised her palms in the air and shrugged her shoulders. "I didn't know."

Nine Months Later

Prior to his scheduled trial, Chris Molina agreed to plead guilty to First Degree Homicide and Robbery in exchange for a life sentence with parole eligibility after forty years. Chris had to agree to testify against Emily Settlemire to get the reduced sentence. Once Emily realized Chris would testify against her, she decided to avoid a public trial and pled guilty. She was not given a reduced sentence for her plea. Both Baxter and Begay attended Emily's sentencing hearing. After a short hearing, the judge sentenced Emily to life in prison with no chance of parole.

After the sentencing, Detectives Baxter and Begay congratulated and thanked each other for their work.

"You never got the other two," said Begay.

"No, but it all worked out," said Baxter. "Justice doesn't always come from a courtroom."

Begay smiled and knew precisely what Baxter meant.